Digital Bedbugs

Digital Bedbugs

2019 Anthology of the Nairobi
Fiction Writing Workshop

Edited by
Makena Onjerika

First published in The Republic of Kenya in 2020 by The Nairobi Fiction Writing Workshop.

Introduction and this compilation copyright © Makena Onjerika 2020
Individual works copyright © the authors 2020

The stories contained in this anthology are entirely works of fiction. The names, characters, and incidents portrayed in them are the works of the authors' imaginations. Any resemblance to actual persons, living or dead, events or localities, is entirely coincidental.

ISBN: 978-9966-138-14-9
Ebook ASIN: B082XFZKPF

The Nairobi Fiction Writing Workshop
P.O. Box 25716 – 00100,
Nairobi, Kenya.

Contents

Introduction

'Digital Bedbugs' is an anthology of work produced at the Nairobi Fiction Writing Workshop in 2018 and 2019. Most of its contributors are Kenyan, but not all. The only criterion for inclusion was the willingness to persevere the gruelling, months-long, re-writing and editing regime. Unity of theme was of little importance, and the stories did not need to limit their setting to Nairobi. It is therefore surprising to me that these stories converse with one another, ploughing over similar thorny landscapes.

They examine and debate police extrajudicial killings and what and who is righteous. They ponder Kenya's various socio-economic classes and the right to enjoy one's earnings when others face economic injustice. They consider how the presence or absence of a parent makes and unmakes the child — strange hereditary troubles haunt these pages. They are perturbed by the powers of the now ubiquitous mobile phone. They are not so sure about sex and its various permutations — beware predatory mothers and suitors who are too good-looking, too rich and too attentive to be true. They expose normalized violence and the ordinariness of its supporters and perpetrators — these are, above all, stories about characters who could be you or me (or maybe not). They dig up past ages to give voice to the dead. They study the various faces of grief. "She said she was sorry for my sadness. I told her I wasn't sad. I was angry," says Sanaa Jabeen's Sonia in 'The Harmonium'.

The search for rest is endless in these stories: rest from pain, rest from loneliness, rest from unwelcome phone calls, rest from music that will not stop, rest from financial distress, rest from bad decisions.

For these writers, corruption of one kind or the other is the invisible monster impinging upon our lives. Olivia Kidula's 'Mummy Dearest' begins with this description of coastal Kenya: "Condom wrappers were intermittently strewn across the sand, and Adam watched in disgusted amusement as a large sand crab rushed by, a used condom glued to its leg, in hot pursuit." While in 'Mariamu', Kiprono Tonui writes: "It is that old liar, he reckoned, and felt reassured because he had fought the devil many times over the years and come out unscathed."

Yet, these stories are not simple struggles between good and bad. More often than not, it is difficult to distinguish between the two, especially inside minds as foggy as the one we inhabit in Shiru Waweru's 'Wife Material'. Black and white slip into grey. As the murderous thug in Sophie Gitonga's 'Where the Bodies are Buried' puts it to the cop: "You and I are the same." And here are the unrepentant words of Kiragu from Shalom Ndiku's 'The Syce': "Bad is the opposite of good… But me, Thuku, I am not bad person. Bad person does something bad when having no reason. Me I had reason. I had very good reason…"

Difficult questions abound, and there are no easy answers to be found in this house, as Tanya discovers in Sheeba Jacob's "Follow the Footpath". Should the persecuted be faulted for using the safe as survival shields? How can what is hereditary be blamed on the individual, so much so, the titular Night Runner in Gladwell Pamba's story begs his wife to never get pregnant by him? And are we responsible for who we become when we live in the stew of unassailable corruption? "It wasn't me who killed the kid," cries the protagonist of Dennis Mugaa's 'Housewarming'.

In Munene Kilongi's 'Digital Bedbugs', we encounter the line "When (a bedbug) bites you that is the moment you realize you are alive and not in a bad dream." These stories will discomfit some. That has always been the outcome of good fiction. For non-Kenyan readers, whole sentences in some stories will seem unattainable. We Kenyan writers live a reality of commingling languages, and there as many Englishes as there were territories of the British Empire. Our worlds will feel strange and off-kilter, but they belong to human reality, and readers who wish to gain entry into them will persevere the bending of their minds. Meanwhile, in these pages, Kenyan readers will face topics our society labels as taboo or distasteful. Reading our work will require strong determination to be creatively free, to throw off mental shackles.

I leave you with this apt sentence from Alvin Kathembe's 'No Good Deed': "(The drink) comes with two little straws to drink out of – every time I take a sip, the alcohol hits my brain as through the barrels of a shotgun". May this be your experience of reading 'Digital Bedbugs'.

January 2020, Nairobi.

Makena Onjerika won the 2018 Caine Prize for African Writing. Her work has appeared or is forthcoming in Fireside Magazine, Wasafari, Waxwing, New Daughters of Africa, Jalada and others. She founded and teaches at the Nairobi Fiction Writing Workshop (NF2W). Connect with her on twitter as @onjerika

Digital Bedbugs

Munene Kilongi

Onyango, a.k.a. Onyi the bossman, sits on a mattress scratching his bushy beard and pondering his fate as he keeps a keen eye on the closed metallic door opposite his bed. It's not a bed in the ordinary sense, but a mattress that buffers his body from the hard, cold floor of the small dingy room he shares with three other men. His balding head is drenched in sweat and glistens as it reflects the glow of a single light bulb hanging high up in the ceiling.

They had breakfast what feels like hours ago. Onyi wolfed down a king-sized breakfast: three fried eggs, toast, sausages, and a mug of black coffee. He and his crew have been waiting ever since, swapping nervous looks as they keep an eye on the door. Has something gone wrong with their scheme?

When the familiar ring of heavy boots plodding towards the door breaks the silence and keys clink, the crew lets out a collective sigh of relief. The steel door unbolts with a loud whizzing sound before a warden the size of a gorilla walks in. His upper body is nearly popping out of his uniform while his thin legs are defiantly flaunting the rules of gravity. He is carrying a gunny bag, which he plunks in the middle of the room then grunts and ambles out of the stuffy room and slams the metallic door behind him. He stomps down the corridor outside and fades into the distance as the crew members retrieve mobile phones and laptops from the gunny bag.

They get to work chap-chap. Onyi's nimble fingers work with vigour on his cell phone as his one eye keeps tabs on data sheets on his laptop screen. Then he makes a call.

"Congratulations! You have just won yourself 150,000 shillings in the ongoing promotion of tuma pesa ushinde by Safaritel," he says before introducing himself. A woman shrieks on the other end of the line.

"Congratulations again, Madam, but there is a small problem," he says. "We have noticed your sim card is registered to two different people and we would like to confirm you are the genuine owner of this number." "How long have you been using our service?" "Oh, ten years, then I think you deserve this prize. Would you kindly furnish me with your sim card's PIN number so we can check that this is the real sim?" He jots down the PIN number on a piece of paper. "Good! We have verified you are the owner of this number, Daktari. How much do you have in your mobile money account so we know if we can send your cash prize to your bank or your mobile money account?" "Thank you. And as a word of caution, never give anyone your mobile money password, even our company employees."

He then instructs her to dial #222222 and follow the commands before politely signing off with a wolfish smile plastered on his face. A new ghost sim card replaces the victim's number, which Onyi has now switched off. He then sweeps the victim's mobile money account clean and forwards the loot to the crew's point man's account.

"I just made us Kshs 23, 000 just like that. And she's a fucking Doctor," Onyi boasts as he high-fives his buddies.

All four men in the room sit cross-legged like Indian gurus hunched over their electronic devices. The room, which is the size of a cubicle, is a former isolation cell for hardcore criminals. The floor is strewn with mattresses except around the ablution area in one corner. The toilet has a leak that makes a persistent drip-drip sound – it irritates the prisoners when the cell is quiet.

Kamande aka Kamze, who's seated next to Onyi, talks to his phone as he sends numerous texts, commanding each to yield returns. Minutes later, there is a beep. He scrolls through the phone and chuckles. "Look at this fool here," Kamze says, as he displays his screen to the rest of the crew.

Please send the money we agreed on to this number (0791852074). My other number has a problem. Please send now! Kamze wrote.

"This fala has just sent me 10k," he says, a wide grin spreading over his beaming face. He forwards the money to the point man.

"Kamze uses juju," says Salim Abubakar, aka Abu, a pudgy guy with chubby cheeks. He still cannot figure out how Kamze makes those jackpot hits. Abu, who's in his mid-forties landed in the bin after swindling a senior government official of millions in a wash-wash deal. His favourite pastime on the outside had been cheque cloning. His men would approach an underpaid or greedy office messenger or accountant, who for a small facilitation fee would take photos of his or her boss' cheques. The messenger/accountant then sent this to Abu's phone and the thing was quickly cloned by a master cheque forger on the notorious River Road at the edges of Nairobi's C.B.D. A National ID card would then be furnished by yet another master forger while the signature on the cheque would be left to the master signatory who walks up and down River Road with ten different types of Biro pens in his pocket. Before the real cheque even left the government office, one of Abu's men would appear at the bank with the fake cheque.

"I am used to big operations that deal with millions, not your kind of amateur league stuff, scamming folks off a few thousands," he brags. Abu's main target is the rich who live off small people's sweat, as he puts it. "It is my national duty to distribute this loot and give employment to jobless people who are supporting families." The crew members know that Abu is a lot of talk and only tolerate him because he still brings in his quota, albeit in humble thousands of shillings, instead of millions.

Brian Okari, aka Brayo, is working on his phone quietly. His kunguru suit has several missing buttons at the belly region and that makes his big tummy tumble out. A thin film of sweat shines around his scalp as he makes calls.

"Hallo!" his deep bass rumbles through the room in the measured notes of a TV presenter. He politely explains his reason for calling as the person on the other end of the line listens keenly. Moments later Brayo is grinning from ear to ear as he sends money to the point man then switches to a new sim card.

"Wow! I have swindled the fool off 60k from his account," he says, his eyes glowing. "If we make money this fast, I believe we'll be able to buy our freedom by next week. That's three months we've been in this cell," he says as he makes another call.

"Try the premium numbers. They don't disappoint," Kamze advises Onyi who now seems to be struggling to get replies. Onyi texts:

Dear customer, your account has been suspended. Call 0762090512 or 0207840506, within 24 hours. KFB BANK.

A panicked man calls back and Onyi engages him in long-winded queries about his supposed account. The anxious victim buys even more airtime to try and get to the root of why his account has been suspended. In no time, Onyi has brought in another 50K.

Everyone in the cell goes still when keys clink outside. The door swings open and Trailer, a scrawny looking fellow with the cunning face of a mongoose and an easy smile that reveals bad dentition, walks in. He is holding trays of fried chicken and chips from KFC, burgers and pizzas. Trailer fist-bumps everyone before commencing his endless stories. A gash above his left eye and a limp in his left leg are badges of honour proclaiming he is a survivor of a lynch mob in the streets of Nairobi. His ill-fitting kunguru outfit is many sizes bigger than him and the slim black and white lines running horizontally across it make him look like a vulture in a zebra's skin. The suit is complemented by a cape that looks more like a floppy chef's hat. At times, when he is standing in his oversized suit and cape, no one knows which way he is facing because he could be walking backwards and still look as if he were walking forwards. In fact, Trailer could walk sideways like a crab and no one would be the wiser.

"Did you get the stuff?" Abu asks Trailer who winks at him and nods.

"In that case, you are welcome to share our meal," Abu says. Trailer is served a huge slab of pizza, a packet of potato chips, and a king-size burger that dwarfs his small frame.

"Eat fast so you don't let us down like last time," Abu says as he turns his attention to the banquet in front of him.

For the next fifteen minutes the only sound is the drip-drip from the faulty cistern intermingled with the raucous symphony of guttural sounds as chicken bones are crushed, burgers chewed and sodas gulped down.

Trailer leaves nothing for the roaches, the ants, and the rats, as he clears every half-eaten morsel on the lunch boxes. After the banquet, everyone lies down on his mattress for a brief siesta.

"What's happening on the other side?" Onyi asks, Trailer, as he stretches himself.

"The prisons commissioner was supposed to make an impromptu check of our facilities today, but something came up and he cancelled the visit," says Trailer.

"How do you know stuff like that?" Kamze asks.

"I'm a big man inside this prison," Trailer says.

"How's your friend, the cook?" Brayo asks.

No one knows Trailer's real name and how he got to work in the kitchen, which is one of the most prestigious duties in the prison. For all his thinness, he eats a plate of mururu meat every day. A Mururu is damn expensive and the cook only takes mobile money, in the very place where being caught with a cell phone can be a death sentence. The sadistic warders clobber and stomp offenders without mercy and many succumb to their injuries. But deals can be made in the prison and prisoners have phones because the cook and the warders will smuggle prohibited stuff to the cells as long as there is money to be made. But if one gets caught by a warder who is not in the deal, the 'friendly' warder will gladly join in pummelling the victim to a pulp. The crew's own operation survives because the commissioner of the prison is in on it, and they bribe a good number of wardens to look the other way when the cook sends them food.

Being a close acquaintance of the cook saves Trailer from the daily fare of scalding hot watery porridge other less lucky prisoners have for breakfast. And the mix of soggy beans and cold crumbling ugali for lunch and supper.

"The cook says hello and thank you for your business," says Trailer.

Some members of the crew suspect Trailer is not paying for his special food in cash or mobile money, for that matter. It's rumoured that cook was once caught fucking an inmate in the bathrooms. Maybe Trailer is cook's wife because he does not qualify to be in the kitchen in the first place. Everyone can see that the mwiko for cooking ugali is taller than Trailer, and he lacks the energy to last 30 minutes turning around huge slabs of wet maize meals for hundreds of hungry prisoners.

Trailer is relaxing in a squat position when he stands up and disappears into the leaky toilet then emerges moments later carrying a condom caked in shit. He carefully wipes shit off the condom with tissue paper before unsealing it and pouring the contents on the floor. There are two packs of cigarettes twisted round and shaped like a screw, new phone sim cards, tiny sachets of coke, and some sticks of weed. All the contraband that is way too valuable to risk trying to smuggle past the wardens who are not part of the crew's payroll. They will demand a few hundred shillings for KFC chicken, but hefty thousands for the stuff in that condom and even more if they learn about the lucrative scams taking place in the isolation cell. And the commissioner will be the first to turn on the crew if word gets out about the scheme. Which is why the gorilla warden confiscates all their equipment before going off duty at six p.m., every evening.

The warden outside bangs his baton on the metal door and peers through the narrow window at the top signalling lunchtime is over, and Trailer should get his ass out of the cell.

"Did you get the spray for bedbugs?" Abu inquires. "The darn things chew me through the night," he says.

"Don't mind about mama," Trailer answers back. "When mama bites you that is the moment you realize you are alive and not in a bad dream." He smiles as he picks up the trash and walks out.

"Trailer has a point," says Onyi. "If you look at the behaviour of a bed bug you will notice we share similarities. The only difference between bed bugs, politicians, and us, is that we are digital bedbugs."

It's amazing that not a single cigarette is broken, thanks to Trailer's professional ass. The crew members get back to work as they light cigarettes, toke weed, and sniff coke.

"I like Trailer," Onyi says.

Abu growls. "You remember that time when the phone he was smuggling in got stuck in his rectum? What about the beating we got from not making quotas? What about that day he couldn't shit and left with all our stuff?"

'But he's persistent and a reliable guy," Onyi insists.

Kamze is feverishly texting: *Hi, I'm fine and I hope you are too. I have a deficit of 30k and my dependant is studying at Nairobi University and is top of her class. She has been discontinued for being out of class for three semesters due to financial challenges. Please help if you can by sending your donation to this number. May God bless you!*

Not thirty minutes later, his phone is ringing like crazy as well-wishers call offering to pay for 'her' fees, hostel accommodation, and meals. He directs them to a paybill number and clocks 300k with that move.

Kamze cut his teeth in a gang in the slums of Kangemi. He specialized in National ID card thefts. His main work in the gang was engaging a target while his colleague smoothly picked the victim's pockets. They then used the ID card to apply for credit cards and make costly purchases or take unsecured loans.

"The guys at the Credit Reference Bureau owe me a lot of money for fetching them thousands of customers, without them breaking a sweat," Kamze says.

After a few hours, the metal door opens again, and the gorilla warden hands Onyi a bottle of Scotch whisky. All activity ceases as everyone pops out his cups — halves of mineral water bottles — and gets his fill of the sweet nectar.

"The commissioner is very happy with your work and says to keep it up," says the warden.

Brayo leans on the wall as he sips his drink. He misses his three children who are all in primary school. A few years back he was working for a reputable company as a social media manager, only to discover it was a money-laundering operation when police showed up to arrest the C.E.O. He lost his job and had to move from a cushy middle-class neighbourhood to the ghettos then finally the slums. Money was short and he was open to any job, and thus got himself swiftly recruited into a quick-money scam.

Tagging along with a woman he barely knew, he scoured for stranded-looking passengers near long-distance bus stations. "We used a drug known as devil's breath," he says. "Sometimes we'd blow the powder at the victim's face or shake their hand and that was it."

His drugged and dazed, zombie victims followed him and the woman to banks and emptied their accounts. At times Brayo and the woman led their victims to deserted alleys, robbed them and left them unconscious.

Later he started an online health insurance company with many financial benefits for cardholders, at the incredible price of 300 bob a month and absolutely free if one convinced five others to join. The pyramid scheme had close to a million members.

"You know, I created a business model that followed Kenya's political philosophy. Feed off the desperate, the vain, and the fools, then discard them when they are worse off than before." The returns were enormous until one day the police turned up at his offices, hidden in a residential housing unit.

Kamze, interrupts Brayo's thoughts with the laughter of a mad man. "I sent this to some dude…" he says, showing them his phone screen.

Hi… am Sandra Johnson, 33 years, Lonely, Single, God-fearing from the United States, working for USAID. Looking for a soulmate to settle in Kenya with. If willing SMS/call this number. Thanks.

I'm Karanja. I am willing, comes the response.

Kamze gets down to formulate a suitable reply, while Onyi receives a rant for a reply to his last text: *Outside here we are eating maize flour full of aflatoxins, milk with heavy metals, sugar with mercury, nyama ya paka ndani ya samosa that's been cooked with generator oil, meat laced with sulphites, githeri cooked with panadol to iva faster…, and you come here trying to con me. If it's soap or milk you want, tell the prison boss to put it on my bill, I will pay through my taxes.*

Everyone laughs. "Umepatikana," they say, slapping Onyi's back.

Then suddenly they hear heavy boots marching towards the door. It opens before they can hide the equipment under their mattresses. A squad of club-wielding warders walks in. Then comes the commissioner, in spectacles, a very sharp black suit and shoes polished to a high shine — the man who sent them the bottle of Scotch Whisky just four hours before. There is another man with him, also in a suit, a politician some of them have seen on T.V.

Before the crew members understand what is happening, they are being stomped and clobbered. They are screaming and begging for their lives.

At the end it, Onyi is the only crew member left conscious. He overhears the commissioner say to the politician, "We will be sure to investigate and find out which wardens were part of this scheme.

I will personally make sure they send back all the money stolen from your daughter."

Onyi passes out. Perhaps he is dead.

Munene Kilongi is a freelance journalist. His work has appeared in One Throne magazine, the Mail and Guardian Newspaper in South Africa, and in international newspapers around the world through Reuters, Associated Press, and McClatchy Newspapers. Connect with him on Twitter as @kilongi.

Follow the Footpath

Sheeba Jacob

Tanya only did it for her mother. India was not part of her itinerary, but her mother talked her into stopping over, after France and before Thailand, for a wedding. Apparently, all of Tanya's family in Kerala would be attending the wedding of the daughter of Tanya's mother's cousin. Tanya tried not to mind; she would be in Thailand soon enough and had registered for a yoga and meditation retreat to help her recover from the looks of pity she knew she would get from her family at the wedding.

In Kerala, she and her mother rented an apartment by the Arabian Sea for the week preceding the wedding. Most of the day, Tanya sat on the balcony, content to look out at the sea, and only went out in the evenings for the short walk to the market around the corner, to get fresh supplies. But as the days passed, Tanya's urge to visit her father's childhood home grew.

She flagged down an auto-rickshaw one morning. After ten miles or so, the city of Ernakulam disappeared and with it, the dense buildings and thousands of people on the streets. The air purified and was easier to breathe. Tanya returned to her childhood drives from the airport to her father's home. There were acres and acres of rice paddy fields on both sides of the road. And from a distance, what looked like a Monet painting: women bent over in the fields wearing wraps on their heads, long-sleeved shirts, and skirts of all different colours. When she counted eight coconut trees in a row, she told the rickshaw driver to make a left, handed him one hundred and fifty rupees and hopped off. She wrapped the dupatta of her bright yellow salwar around her neck, using the corner to wipe off the inevitable sweat. She walked about two hundred feet and finally reached the steps of the house.

The house was a typical Kerala home, made of teak wood with a stone courtyard at its centre. When she was a little girl, she used to walk barefoot on the floors inside, loving the jingle of her silver anklets as she danced on the cool marble floor. She could already smell the jasmine trees around the courtyard's perimeter, and the smell triggered memories. Even when Tanya was in the States, all her father had to do was mention Kerala, and she would be brought back to his home and this scent.

These days, a distant uncle and his family occupied the house. Through the open curtains of the living room window, Tanya noted several changes as she went to ring the doorbell. A fifty-five-inch television screen and garish modern furniture clashed with the fine-polished wood ceilings and the classical architecture of the house. Paintings from artists like Raja Ravi Verma had been displaced by reproduced photographs of the Eiffel Tower and boats in Venice.

A man with a bushy moustache came to the door. "Ah, you must be Tommy Uncle's daughter," he said.

This was Prasad Uncle. She greeted him politely, shaking her head side to side in typical Malayalee fashion. She said she was very happy to meet him, although she felt no familial connection with him.

"Please, come in, come in," he said as if she were a next-door neighbour dropping by for a visit.

Tanya had no interest in making small talk, but it would have been rude to not drink the coffee his wife made, with two extra spoons of sugar and eat at least one piece of overly sweet fruit cake. As she sat in a house where she had spent several summers as a child, she felt both strong familiarity and great distance. She peered into the courtyard where she and several cousins had played for hours upon hours, inventing all kinds of games. Her cousin Nadia and she had convened meetings on the stairs – the first agenda always being to read Filmfare magazines and then create the scenes they showcased at family talent nights, pretending to be Shahrukh and Kajol. The courtyard now had a small swing set and basketball hoop. She had imagined the smell; all the jasmine trees were gone.

"So, what brings you here?"

"I thought I should visit dad's home since we spent so much time here during our summers when I was younger."

Her uncle nodded but put most of his attention towards following the BBC news on that godforsaken television.

She tried a different approach. "Dad used to tell me wonderful stories of his childhood in this house. Did you grow up around here too?"

"No, we lived in Dubai and never made it back home. It wasn't until I was given the rights to this land that I could finally transform it into something more, you know, modern."

Tanya drank her coffee and kept down an expletive.

"And you, what are you doing now?" asked Prasad Uncle.

Tanya had to think through her response ever so carefully. One answer could potentially create awkward silence, or worse, lead to a lecture. The other response was what all Indian uncles and aunties could easily compartmentalize into that part of their brains that checked off the success boxes. She decided to give the curated response.

"I'm a lawyer in Chicago."

"Aah. Very good."

She gulped the last of the coffee and placed the cup on the glass table. She could almost hear the laughter from when her family played games of gin rummy sitting around the huge wooden table her great grandfather had built over a century before. If tables could talk.

"What happened to the wooden table, Uncle?" she asked.

"We sold it immediately. We didn't need this house to look like a 19th-century museum."

Tanya was officially done with this conversation. She stood up from the uncomfortable steel chair and asked her uncle if it would be okay for her to go to the veranda. She felt as if there was something waiting for her there.

The last time she had been on the veranda was with her father when she was fourteen years old. She had always found this part of the house somewhat mystical, especially early in the morning. The Hindu temple was only one mile down the road. The Catholic Church was not too much further. The devotional prayers from both began at five a.m. and woke the village from its slumber. There was dew on the grass and a thin humidity in the air that made everything seem to breathe. Hibiscus flowers in the trimmed bushes around the veranda opened their colourful skirts while tendrils of vines curled up the poles of the house.

On that last morning when Tanya was on the veranda with her father, the air was cooler than usual. They had both woken up at four a.m. because of jetlag. The moon still shone in the West. Tanya's dad brought out two cups of coffee, and they drank slowly as they watched Johnny, the toddy tapper, climb up the nearby palm tree to retrieve the fermented liquor that made everyone happier in the evenings.

"I called this place home for twenty years of my life… I owe everything I am to this place," her father said, suddenly. He had a bookish look when he wore his thick, black-framed glasses.

She thought to herself, who would have guessed that a small boy from India would end up a lepidopterist studying swallowtail butterflies from South Asia.

"Papilio liomedon," she whispered under her breath.

"Why butterflies, Dad?" she asked that morning, realizing, strangely, that she had never asked before.

Tanya's father put his coffee cup down on the stool between them and wrapped his cashmere shawl around his neck. He narrowed his eyes at Johnny in the tree.

"Growing up, your grandfather was rarely home because he needed to provide for all eight of us. Your grandmother lost two children to malaria and polio and suffered from a powerful depression. For several years, she would go into her bedroom and not come out for two or three days. I desperately wanted to cure her. As her youngest and closest, I almost spiralled like her — it was an easy way to deal with the pain of her abandonment. But something saved me: wonder, a deep sense of wonder," he looked at Tanya meaningfully. "I saw light in the smallest of moments and things. And what is more wondrous than this?" He stretched out his hand to a butterfly floating near them. They always seemed to find him, as though they knew he was a friend.

Tanya sat on the veranda, now alone, trying to remember every detail of that morning.

"Wonder," she whispered.

Stories from his childhood had always felt like a blanket that settled warmly on her shoulders. Her father did have a sense of awe that never left him. And he did everything he could to love Tanya's mother and her the way his own mother could not love him. His family often made fun of him of his career, but he was one of the most sought-after lepidopterists in America.

She had been eighteen years old when he had passed away. In the first year, she had vivid dreams about him. She felt that although he had left the material world, he was close to her. She spoke to him as if he were right there. Perhaps it was this assurance about his presence that made her stop talking to him, hurrying through life, until she was suddenly twenty-eight years old with a cancer diagnosis hanging over her head. And then he was no longer there. Throughout her chemo, she did everything to try and communicate with him. She read through journal entries, looked at old photo albums, watched home videos. Nothing. When she spoke to him, she felt nothing.

If only she had just told her father how proud she was of him. When she was younger, she was embarrassed to tell her friends that her father studied butterflies. Her friends' parents had normal jobs like doctors, engineers and accountants. It was already hard enough being the daughter of immigrants in America. She desperately wanted to choose a path in life that would earn her respect and make her well-known instead of obscure. Now, with a successful career behind her, she could not feel more obscure and odd. She realized that her father had figured it out: doing something purposeful and meaningful with his whole heart, instead of caring what others thought.

Well, dad, I'm here. Do you think the family will like my tattoo and haircut? She laughed at her own joke.

Her shirt was drenched from her hour of waiting on the veranda. She felt nothing even close to wonder. And she felt nothing of her father. The April heat in Kerala was like an ominous truth, silent and brooding. She noticed her uncle's wife staring at her through the window when she slipped off the dupatta and her sleeveless kurta top revealed several flowers blooming on her right arm.

That look left Tanya feeling exhausted and ready to leave India. She did not want to face her relatives and all the judgement at the wedding the next day. She did not want to care what they thought, but she did. She cared too much, she always did. She said her goodbyes to Prasad Uncle. She intended to get back to the rental, pack and fly out to Thailand or walk there, if she had to.

The rickshaw driver appeared to have picked a route home with the worst possible congestion. Tanya had to cover her mouth and nose with her dupatta from all the toxic fumes that crept inside the open vehicle. All the purity she had felt on her way to her dad's house was replaced with a heavy and dirty fog. Why had she thought she could find answers in a house?

Before the surgery, Tanya had not minded standing out in a crowd and especially showing off her cleavage – padded bras, subtly cut shirts. She loved being a B cup. There was enough there to make her feel she had decent sex appeal, but not too much. Peter always made that clear to her, especially when they were both naked.

After the surgery, Tanya could not have cared less about her phantom flesh. The doctor offered to reconstruct her breasts at an even larger size than before. During the consultation, Peter's eyes opened wide and he nodded in support. Tanya wasn't having it — the chemo, the surgery, the months and months of not knowing how things would pan out — she wanted a reminder of who she had become.

The divorce had been painful. She noticed several months after the surgery that Peter couldn't look her in the eyes while they lay together. He had this panicked look on his face — almost as if he were trapped.

Several times, he had tried to convince her to wear the silicone inserts the doctor had given her when they went out or when she wore a bathing suit. Once, when they took a trip to the Dominican Republic with a few friends, she saw Peter squirm and turn red after she took off her tank top at the bench.

He turned out to be far less adaptable than she had given him credit for — sure, he prided himself in summiting the 14,000-foot glacier on Mt. Rainier during challenging weather — but he had the emotional backbone of a flea.

The rickshaw driver dropped her off at the apartment. She noticed how he stared at her too like she was a freak show. Why couldn't people just say what they were thinking?

It was too hot. She was hardly in the mood for packing just then and was more than grateful when she unlocked the door of the rental and found two frosty drinks on the table.

"Mom, since when do you drink margaritas and how did you find them here in Cochin?"

Her mother was deep-frying vadas at the stove. She wore a long nightie and had her hair tied up in a bun. She still looked like a young university student, even at the age of sixty-five.

"I have my ways. You know, Priti Aunty and I go every Thursday to Casa de Mexico for happy hour."

"What? Really? Do you both get drunk? I can't even imagine. You wouldn't let me come near a drink until I was twenty-five years old. You used to give me such judgy eyes when I got a second one."

"I'm sixty-five years old. I deserve a little fun in my life!" She did a little salsa move while sipping her margarita.

Tanya felt laughter trickle up her throat but managed only a smile. Her mom did deserve fun in her life. Losing a husband and having a daughter diagnosed with cancer within ten years of each other was not for the faint of heart. And while her mom always seemed to have a positive attitude, Tanya knew she struggled quietly and mourned privately. Whenever Tanya visited her and found her eyes bloodshot, her mother immediately blamed her bad allergies.

"Feeling ready for this wedding, Tanya?"

"Hmmm, let me think about that, mom. Seeing extended family one year after the divorce and two years after battling cancer? Sounds like the perfect reunion!"

"Okay, that's one way to look at this. But how about meeting your aunties and uncles? They aren't getting any younger. Your little cousins adore you too. And of course, Priya is getting married tomorrow."

Her mom casually popped a fried vada in her mouth.

Tanya scrutinized her. "Excuse me, mom. Can you repeat that last part again?"

"Priya is getting married." She took another swig of the margarita.

"Oh, right! Priya, your distant cousin's daughter. I know how much this wedding must mean to you."

Tanya took a gulp of the margarita herself and narrowed her eyes at her mother, realizing something.

"What? Why are you giving me that look, Tanya? Listen, you know what they say: when you are single, you must be willing to mingle."

"Really mom, that's what they say?"

If she were not so flustered, Tanya would have immediately typed her mom's latest idiom into her phone, in the reminder's page meant for mom-permutations of classic sayings:

Tanya, money doesn't grow on mango trees.

C'mon, you think I was reincarnated yesterday?

Okay, girl. We can cross that footpath when we get to it.

"Mom, I was married for five years of my life. I probably enjoyed only half of that time. Forty per cent of my friends are divorced. Why do you want me to rush into another relationship?"

"Because I think you can find someone who will treat you as you deserve."

"Don't you get it, mom? Your marriage to dad was an anomaly. I promise you, men like dad don't exist."

"C'mon, Tanya. You can't believe that."

Two years ago, when Peter had been on a work trip, her mom had stayed with her. This was soon after her double mastectomy. When she got out of the shower, she looked at her reflection in the mirror: she had no hair, no eyebrows and no breasts. At first, the tears came slowly. And then she started to weep. She hadn't cried once since the diagnosis, but within ten minutes, she had fallen to the floor unable to control herself.

Her mother came in, took a towel, wrapped Tanya up and rocked her back and forth as she whispered, over and over, "You don't even know how strong you are." Peter couldn't soothe her even half as much as her mother did that night.

Several of her friends had gone through divorces. Most of them came out looking like they had fought in World War III. She wanted to be one of those divorcees who walked into a room and everyone thought to themselves, *Damn, Tanya has done good for herself getting rid of him!* One of her aspirations after leaving Peter was to become a DILF. And more importantly, a cancer-survivor-ILF.

Her mother took her hand. "No, mollae. You will find what your father and I had... I know you will." She went twirling around the kitchen and salsa-stepping.

Tanya drunk the rest of her drink in one gulp. Her mother, the one who had always been full of anxiety about her life, seeing obstacles to be surmounted and traps to be avoided, had slowly morphed into her father, the eternal optimist, but still, Tanya would have preferred having them both and things as they once were.

✝

The following day, she was yet again drenched in sweat, and at the request of her mother, wore a heavy kanchipuram silk sari to try impress possible suitors at Priya's wedding. She'd taken a selfie before leaving the rental apartment and texted her best friend Matty, *Sweating the dream out here.*

There were over one thousand people expected to come, but the church ceremony would be much smaller, around four hundred people. On the way to the wedding in the taxi, Tanya put on a bit of lipstick and a gold bindi on her forehead, in preparation for the hoards. She always felt herself an imposter when wearing Indian clothing, especially thick silk saris. Today, even more than usual, she knew she would stand out. After years and years of long, lustrous hair that cascaded down her back and fitting the script of what an Indian woman 'should' look like, the perfect box she'd thought she'd created had fallen apart at the corners. Who do you become when all that you were doesn't exist anymore?

Tanya's mother always had this grace to her, especially dressed in a sari. She knew how to walk and laugh and just be. Tanya was an awkward giraffe, always terrified of needing the bathroom. Her purse was full of safety pins.

Her own wedding had been small, about a hundred and fifty people. Peter and she decided to get married at Big Sur right on the beach. The cliffs were rugged, but the water was calm. She wore a crown of flowers in her hair and a sleeveless white dress. She worked very hard to look like a bohemian bride and grew her hair a few extra inches below her midback for the role. People came up to her to tell her how stunning she looked and how the two of them were such a beautiful couple. She remembered the feeling of the sand under her feet – cool and refreshing. She had felt so safe with Peter that day. Two years ago, she had gone to Miami with a few friends. The sand had almost burned her feet.

As they arrived at the church, Tanya put on her perma-smile and got out to hug hundreds of relatives. They all told her how beautiful she looked and how she should always wear a sari. Tanya had an uncanny ability to tell when people were lying. There was something about the intonation of their voice and the way they raised their eyebrows that put her back into a Law and Order courtroom: Guilty! she thought to herself. Liar! But compliments are the glue of a polite Kerala society, so she couldn't say anything except, "Oh thank you, Aunty," and "Thank you, Uncle."

The ceremony was to take place in an hour or so and the reception was right next door. After about the twentieth empty hug, she noticed a car pull up outside, and her cousin Nadia exited with her husband and children. Nadia who had once been more than a sister. Watching her tidy her children, Tanya remembered a conversation they had heard years ago. She'd called from the States to tell Nadia about Peter and how she thought he was the one. Nadia started crying on the other end.

"Don't get me wrong," she said. "You know from the bottom of my heart how happy I am for you. It's just, when you get married, I'll be single… and alone."

Tanya had made a huge effort in the first few years of her marriage to call Nadia monthly and check-in on her.

Now, Nadia slowly walked towards her on the sandy pathway. She wore a periwinkle sari with a sleeveless blouse. Her hair had golden brown highlights and was the same length as Tanya's when she had gotten married.

"You look great," Nadia said holding the hands of her two children. She had this look on her face, the classic cancer pity-guilt look. "I'm sorry I never got in touch with you during everything you went through. Things just got so busy with the kids and work. But honestly, if there is anything you need while you're here, please let me know."

Tanya cringed. How could someone who once felt like a sister suddenly feel so foreign to her? She'd never understood the 'Things just got so busy' line. She wished people could just say, "I didn't know what to say to you when you first got diagnosed and then as time passed, I did a shitty job of keeping in touch. Now that I see you face-to-face, I really have no excuse. I'm so sorry."

"You don't have to make excuses. I just wish I heard from you. Of all people, I needed you the most."

Nadia's eyes filled with tears as she whispered, "I'm so sorry."

Tanya had to walk away. As she approached the back of the church, she saw a father playing with his daughter among the pews. The girl was no older than six or seven years old. The father was throwing her up in the air and catching her. The little girl was giggling, so innocent and trusting, without any doubt that her father would catch her.

"Tanya, do you want to go higher?"

"Yes!"

"Are you sure? Even higher?"

"Yes!"

Tanya felt overwhelming hopelessness. "Mom, I'm going for a walk."

"Okay, mollae. The ceremony should begin at ten-thirty am."

Tanya walked out to the church courtyard and turned right because she noticed there was a small footpath there. She walked and walked, following the footpath. The bottom of her sari picked up dust and bits of dust, but she couldn't care less. What was she

35

doing with her life? She'd never blamed her circumstances on the cancer, but today, she kept thinking to herself, Why me? Really God. Why me? All the plans she'd had: the civil rights career, the three kids with Peter, a house in Carmel, her happily ever after.

And now: no career, no husband, and definitely no chance of having biological kids.

At the end of the footpath, on the banks of a river, and because she could go no further, she shook her fists in the air and screamed, "What was your plan? Was it all a big joke for you?"

Feeling a bit faint, she crouched near a palm tree for some shade. And for the second time in many years, she cried. She cried for her lost marriage, she cried for her lost breasts, she cried for her lost femininity, she cried for her lost father, she cried for her lost children. She surprised herself with how many tears she had within her. The loss swallowed her and for a moment, she wished the earth would too. She buried her head between her knees and voluminous silk, willing everything away.

She felt some rain on her arms, a few raindrops. Then slowly, there was a pattering on her head. She kept her head down, wanting the rain to beat down on her. But while the intensity of the raindrops increased, she noticed she wasn't getting wet. She could hardly open her eyes from all her crying, but when she did, she closed them again and opened them slowly, because she couldn't believe what she saw: a sea of blue and green.

There were hundreds of butterflies at first. And then as she stood up, thousands of butterflies surrounded her. She felt it: wonder. She felt about to overflow. Closing her eyes again, she let the butterflies touch her with their softness. And so many memories came flooding back, like how during elementary school, her father and her put their shoes on at the same time using two different shoe horns before he took her to school or how he made her coffee every day during her final exams in high school and wrote her notes to inspire her to do her best. Little by little, she felt a release, something heavy leaving her body and the emptiness filling up with joy.

Welcome home, dad. We have so many things to catch up on.
She laughed as she had not done in years.

Sheeba Jacob is an educator, singer-songwriter and mom. While her home is in Los Angeles with her husband and son, she has lived on four continents and attributes her creativity to the many worlds she has seen (and a good cup of coffee every morning). Connect with her on Instagram as sheeba1012 and Facebook as sheebamariemusic.

Housewarming

Dennis Mugaa

L isten, I know how this sounds, but it wasn't me who killed the kid. There are things you may have heard people say about me: Wafula is a liar, Wafula is a thief, Wafula is a cheat, and Wafula is a killer. I am all these things except a killer.

Now that I am about to receive my sentencing, I should clear up a few things because, given the way this trial has gone, I doubt anyone understands that I was only housewarming.

First, I need to explain about Chege. Nine years ago, I was released from prison. Before you get any ideas, I should add that I got there by mistake. The system is flawed, you see, although by the time I realized this, I was already behind bars.

In 2005 or was it 2006 — I forget now — I got a job at the Treasury, as a junior clerk, a senior assistant to the Minister. I was what you would call a 'going-places person'. How I got that job, after years of job seeking in vain, is a mystery to me now, because in this country you always have to know people to get anything, and I didn't know anyone important. But back then, how I got the job didn't bother me much. I was a smart guy, after all, with a decent degree from the University of Nairobi.

My job involved simply doing whatever the Minister told me to do; basically, I was second in command in the Ministry.

Later that year the Anglo-Leasing corruption scandal hit the news. You must have heard of it. The media made such a furore over it and ran headlines like 'Runaway Corruption' and 'Stop the Flow'. You know, dramatic words from self-righteous people. My favourite was 'Treasury Terror' – I liked how it rhymed. But it was nothing. People steal all the time in government, so I didn't understand why everyone was getting so worked up. It's not like anyone had died.

Still, the way Kenya works, someone needed to go to prison over it. Let's just say that, somehow, that person ended being me.

Many things happened to me in prison. Things you might want to hear about. But I don't have time to tell you about them, because the judge is going to appear at that desk any minute now. Let me jump to Chege, my cellmate the last year I was in prison.

There was nothing, absolutely nothing, remarkable about Chege. No, I need to be more precise. He was average in all attributes: height, weight and age. I am the complete opposite: tall, big and very smart. People envy me for it, I know. But I forgot to mention that even people's attitude towards Chege was average; it bordered on apathy.

At first, I felt that way about him too. But then this guy told me what had landed him in prison, and I could not believe it.

One night, a few months before my time in prison was over, Chege and I were in our cell and I couldn't sleep. I felt Chege awake in the dark – a man can always tell when another man isn't sleeping;

it's an intuitive thing Chege and I had. So I asked the question, just out of curiosity.

"I used to be a taxi driver." He stopped and cleared his throat, and I started to think that he was truly retarded because he wasn't making any sense, you know. Since when was driving taxis a crime? But then I thought maybe he murdered people in his taxi and wished I hadn't asked him. The thing is, I hate blood. Just thinking about it makes my stomach-ache immediately. You see how it couldn't have been me who killed the kid?

So Chege cleared his throat and then he said the most incredible thing: "I used to drive people to the airport, and then I would go back to their houses and take their things. It went well... for three or so years, but one day I drove this lady to the airport, then after about an hour, she came back because she had forgotten her passport, and found me taking her television. She screamed, and by the time I was brought to court, the police had added assault to the charge sheet." He kept quiet after that and fell asleep.

I, on the other hand, was sleepless that whole night, simply because I couldn't believe the simple genius of the idea. You see it, right?

The funny thing about prison is you go in an innocent man, and when you come out, you are exactly what the court said you were. They released me, and I became a conman.

After we had been friends for some time, Chege told me about all these cons that he wanted to start when he got out. His favourite person to talk about was Victor Lustig who, in the mid-twenties, apparently managed to sell the Eiffel Tower – I forget now if it was once or twice, but the point Chege was trying to make was obvious. 'Con' is in the word 'confidence', after all.

I decided to be confident and started implementing Chege's ideas; he was still inside and didn't need them, you see.

There was this beautiful one, beautiful because of its simplicity. It involves buying things from online market spaces like OLX. The thing you want to steal is literally brought to you. So when the seller arrives with it, preferably in a semi-crowded street in the C.B.D., you pretend to have a look at it and then you run.

Another one involves dropping coins in matatus. It has to be coins you drop and in a Public Service Vehicle, whether a Nissan or a bus, doesn't matter. The key thing here is to look poor so your clothes have to be dishevelled and your hair unkempt, so that the passenger next to you feels pity for you when you ask him or her to pick the coins up for you. And when he or she is doing that, you reach for his or her wallet and alight at the next stop, before anyone notices.

I won't get into any other cons since the judge is here and we are all rising to show respect. But the thing about any con is that once you fool a few people, word gets out, and your clientele shrinks by the day. You have to be creative every day. It's not a long-term kind of thing.

Thankfully, Chege was released before I ran out of ideas. The first thing he did when he got out was to come to see me because he had heard I was making it big. He congratulated me on implementing his ideas. Of course, he thought he was the genius of us two.

The second thing he did was buy a car and go back to being a taxi driver. I never asked where he got the money for the Nissan Note. He didn't drive anywhere else in Nairobi, just to and from the airports. And what was even stranger, he didn't go back to stealing. I thought he had to be making money through some other scheme he was not telling me about. Or maybe airport transport really did bring in good money.

I wasn't making much money, myself. A few months after Chege was released, my landlord kicked me out of my bedsitter, and I had nowhere to sleep, so I called Chege. He said he was at the airport, dropping a client.

I had been thinking of begging him for some money, but suddenly, I had an even better idea.

"How long is he gone for?" I asked, and at this, I heard Chege make a sound like he was being strangled; he didn't talk for a few seconds.

"I just want to stay at his place, bana," I said.

Chege laughed. He was still laughing when we met up later on.

"Oh, you're serious," he said when I asked about the house again.

"The other option is me staying with you, boss."

"No, no, my wife will refuse. I'm a changed man, and my wife knows you from the prison visits."

We were silent on the way to his client's house. The man had left for Addis Ababa and would be gone for about a week. When I got into his house, I quickly realised that he was a bachelor.

It's an easy thing to get into people's houses, by the way, too easy if you ask me. They use these flimsy locks, and I have been picking locks since high school. Back then it had been just for fun, now it was a professional necessity, like computer literacy on a C.V. And neighbours don't care nowadays: no one ever notices anything.

"He comes back in five days," Chege said, but he looked frightened. He must have thought that he was making a mistake.

"Don't worry, I'll keep the house warm for him," I said to Chege, but he only gave me an uneasy smile and walked away.

That night I slept there and the next and the next, until Chege told me he was on the way to pick the client up from the airport.

Here is the surprising part: when the client showed up, he noticed nothing at all. Nothing. Or maybe he did and never told Chege. Who knows?

I realized it was possible to live rent-free in Nairobi. And I wasn't even stealing anything.

The rules for housewarming, if you ever want to do it, are quite simple:

1. Don't take anything at all. Leave everything as you found it, even the trash and dust.
2. Make sure the whole family is away, or better still, house warm only for people who live alone.
3. Don't be seen by the building management or the guards, if it's an apartment building.

After I explained these rules to Chege, he stopped being nervous. Once, he and I even slept in an N.G.O. boss's house in Runda. It's funny, you know, because this is the kind of place you expect maximum security, and there wasn't even a guard. The guy had gone to Somalia to observe the elections there and had given his entire staff days off.

This was the only time Chege and I broke some of my housewarming rules. We drank a few of the guy's wines, but that was okay because he had a whole room of them.

✝

I must now tell this story faster because the prosecution had started on its closing arguments against me. I wish the prosecutor would stop pointing at me. I really did not kill that kid.

At some point, a year or so after I began housewarming, Chege took this family of three to the airport. They were going to the United States for three months. They lived in an apartment in Madaraka, close to Strathmore University. I went to their apartment, about an hour after they had left. By this time, I had become a pro and knew I could get away with saying I was so-and-so's cousin, keeping the house warm until they returned — as long as no one took my photo and the building had no CCTV cameras, I was free to walk around and enjoy life.

This was how I met the kid. He was the family's neighbour. He was about twenty years old and went to school at the university.

That first time he walked past me with his chin tucked into his chest and dragging his feet along as if he was falling.

"Sup, I'm Tony, you're new, right, you can call me T," he said.

Tony (I refuse to call him T) wanted to be a musician. He said he wanted to do Hip-hop and that the Kenyan music industry needed fresh blood, and the only real musician out there was Fanaka. He didn't tell me any of this though, I heard him through the walls between our apartments. And I only heard him because he had parties all the time. He had them in the morning, in the afternoon, in the evening. On every occasion he made people listen to his music. It's not like I want to spit on the dead, but his music was bad. It was so bad that even I knew it was bad, and I'm not a huge fan of music. Mostly I listen to Oliver Mtukudzi or Papa Wemba, off cassette tapes, old school style.

The other songs Tony played at his parties were quite good, but those ones were not his. He also had a bad taste in friends. I heard them complain about his food. I mean when someone comes to your house, she shouldn't complain about the food you give her. One time someone stole his television remote controller, and another time someone used the toilet and left without flushing, and things like that. See, I didn't mind their conversations, but the noise when they played music got in the way of my sleep. I tried to tell him to keep it down the first week.

"Yes, sawa sawa I will," he said and then he went and added the volume.

One day I went into his house when he was in school and cut the wires of his stereo, but the kid came back and bought new ones.

"These rats," he said.

I wished I could call his father or mother to deal with him. I also wished that he would die... but that was once, and only once, when I was asleep, and he woke me up with his stupid noise. Anyone would have thought along those lines, at two am: it's not an admission of guilt or anything.

So here is the part you won't believe, but it's true. After a month or so, another musician came to live in the apartment next to mine. I began thinking of telling Chege to find me a new place to live because I was now living between musicians, but a day later I realised that the new musician was — and even I still don't believe it — Fanaka!

The kid, Tony, didn't know how to act anymore, because his idol was now his neighbour. He started showing up at Fanaka's house, every day. The first day he went to say hello as a neighbour. Fanaka received him well that day, and I heard them chatting about music outside Fanaka's door. The next day Tony brought Fanaka his music. Mixtape, he called it. All the while I was thinking that Fanaka wouldn't listen to more than a minute of it.

I would find out a bit later that Fanaka was having financial difficulties and had moved from Karen to Madaraka to cut down on costs. His music wasn't doing that well, and it wasn't good either, in my opinion. It sounded like the kid's music, but see, somehow Fanaka was famous. Maybe because Fanaka was the opposite of Tony, in a lot of ways.

He was a private person: he didn't speak much in his house. I only used to hear the television when he was home. And he was home most of the time; only his wife went to work. She came back in the evening and dropped her car keys in a bowl.

"Why didn't you go to the studio?" she asked him.

"The hit song I'm working on will be the song of the year."

"That boy asked me about you again on the stairs."

"Don't mind him."

Tony told a friend he wanted to own something of Fanaka's, even his autograph, just basically anything that he could find. A bit of an obsession, I thought.

One good thing that happened was now Tony stopped having the parties. Maybe he was afraid of pissing off his idol, you know. It was so quiet; I was finally able to read 'How to Win Friends and Influence People' and '48 Laws of Power'. I was even thinking of retiring from housewarming and becoming a motivational speaker.

But things went wrong. Fanaka never listened to Tony's music. And Tony in return kept on knocking at his door during the day when his wife wasn't around. Then he started hovering near Fanaka's car hoping to catch him. Fanaka spoke to the building management, and Tony was cautioned, of course. But all through this, he kept telling any friend who visited, "The music industry has to change, mimi ndio future."

So one evening, about two months into housewarming, Fanaka went to the studio. I was in the kitchen cutting up some vegetables. Fanaka had left the door to his house unlocked. Now I know a lot of people keep asking how I knew the door was unlocked. It's simple. I didn't hear his keys in the lock. So, I went and checked that his car was gone, then I entered his house, just to see how a music superstar lives. I got comfortable on his couch, which is how I left my sweater there, by mistake, and by the way, don't you think it shameful that the prosecution used it as evidence against me?

Anyway, after I left Fanaka's, Tony suddenly turned up the volume on his music player. Just like that, after a month of silence. Then he walked past my window, headed towards Fanaka's. I thought he would do what he always did: knock at the door then sit on the stairs sulking. But no, that day Tony found the door unlocked and walked in. He put his mixtape in Fanaka's stereo, and I heard its horrible sound through the walls. So that was two apartments booming that music and me between them. But it wasn't late yet, so I decided not to mind too much.

I was still cooking when Fanaka and his wife came home. Apparently, he had just gone to pick her up.

"What are you doing!" I heard him shout at Tony.

The kid ran. Fanaka chased after him punching him.

"Usirudi tena! Nyangau!"

They ran down the apartment's corridor. I rushed out but forgot I had a knife, the one I was using in the kitchen. Tony ran past me towards the corridor's guard rails. He jumped before Fanaka could reach him. I raced down to the ground floor to see if he was okay. He wasn't. But I noticed that he was wearing my sweater, so I tried to remove it from him first. The building's security guard found me at it.

"What are you doing?" he asked.

"That is my sweater," I said, before realizing I was holding the knife.

†

The guard and Fanaka became prosecution witnesses and swore I stabbed the kid. Fanaka released a song dedicated to Tony. It's a hit song now. I don't like it because it sounds too much like Tony's music, but the message is good.

The Judge is saying something. I try to hear, but my ears are ringing.

"The accused shall receive the maximum penalty for the crime of murder." The courtroom is silent, and then cameras start clicking at me. "The court sentences the accused, Joseph Wafula, to death."

Dennis Mugaa has been shortlisted for the K & L Prize for African Literature and is a former Ebedi fellow. His previous work has appeared in The Kalahari Review.

Mariamu

Kiprono Tonui

On Monday evening, he drove his white Toyota Probox home from the local trading centre, packed full of neighbours. When he arrived at his gate, his passengers alighted as he was going no further. He detoured off the main road and onto a dirt track home. Lightness of heart stole over him as the late evening wind lapped his face and soothed his nostrils.

He was home.

He changed clothes for his evening walk. He donned a T-shirt, brown khaki trousers, a light coat and a flat cap on his head — to ward off mosquitoes in case he was delayed in the fields — and took his walking stick. He walked out with a flourish.

He lingered at the cattle pens and assessed the tea bushes and a field of maize plants in the lower side of his smallholding. He was satisfied that all was well.

The grass crackled beneath his feet as he crossed a lonely ridge on the farm, headed for home, and then he stopped by his earthen dam and surveyed the dark marks left by the receding water.

The water is running out, he thought, surveying the sky. A sliver of moon was just emerging shyly from behind a turf of cloud. He realized the rains were imminent and would probably arrive just before the full moon.

He thought he heard the crunch of dry leaves.

It must be one of the farmhands, he thought. His workers, housed within the farm, came to draw water or bathe late at night, after a day's work.

He could make out a ghostly figure and presently a soft voice issued forth.

"Is it well with you, Reverend?"

"It is well," he mumbled and squinted. It was his neighbour from across the upper ridge.

She was carrying a bundle of wood and a water-can. His nostrils picked out light lemon notes he associated with a common soap brand whose name he could not recall just then, and this told him she must have been from bathing in the stream below, after a day's work at one of the expansive farms. Her name was Mariamu Cheleel and she resided in her parents' home and subsisted on odd jobs to fend for herself and two children. She had been in class eight with his eldest daughter and could not proceed with her education due to a lack of school fees. In a moment of heady teenage experimentation, she had been put in the family way by a herds boy from a neighbouring farm, and as was the norm then, she had been married to him shortly after. But the marriage had not lasted; he treated her cruelly.

After a particularly nasty bout of domestic violence — he fractured her leg with a chebunyo, a knobkerrie so named after the market it was bought from — her ageing father forbade her from ever again stepping foot in her matrimonial home, lamenting that he had not received any form of bride price, anyway.

The Reverend recalled her occasional presence in the Church; he was sure she never missed the Easter and Christmas services.

"Eei, it is late for you," he said, as she unloaded her bundle.

"Yes. I was trying to clear a weedy patch before the rains." Her voice rose gently.

"Mmm… the long rains season will soon begin; the warm nights do not lie." He looked at the silvery night sky with its grotesque clouds that hugged the heavens like monsters.

Awkward silence reigned.

She leaned forward and brought her arms together and this pressed her breasts and created cleavage. Was she doing it consciously? He noticed that the loose dress she was wearing for the fields had an unnecessarily low neckline. He fidgeted. "Goodnight," he said, averting his gaze from her bosom.

"Eeh Reverend…" she said.

"Yes…"

It was getting late. What did she want to talk about at such an hour, in the dark?

"Do you still need vibaruas to weed your farm? I am willing to weed an acre since I have finished the portion I have leased over there."

Surely, she knew his wife dealt with the daily running of the farm.

"Come in the morning and we can survey the portions left."

"It is well then. Goodnight."

He absentmindedly watched the rise and fall of her firm, rounded buttocks as she vanished into the night.

She came early the next morning, catching him in the act of shaving, in a vest, seated outside the house with a mirror and a basin of warm water. He had forgotten about her.

"Rachel! Rachel!" he bawled across the veranda towards the chicken run which sat on the edge of the compound. Presently, a stout woman emerged, holding a feeding pan in her hands, her clothing daubed white. She was a big woman, her face bronzed by the tropical sun, but the round and homely face retained traces of the beauty that had attracted him to her long ago. She noticed their neighbour and took long deliberate steps towards them.

The women exchanged pleasantries.

"She is seeking work. Are there any portions left in the maize fields?"

"Only one portion in the upper farm is left."

They haggled over price for a while and settled on a payment of three thousand shillings per acre.

He then departed for his shop in the local trading centre where he kept himself busy. He really did not need the money, but the extra money was handy in retirement. The church paid him a little stipend for the services he had rendered over the years. He had started as a Lay Leader, but risen through the ranks, on Theological Education by Extension, to the position of Reverend, just before he retired.

In those early days, the crop was ripe in the fields, but the workers were few. He was among the first converts to Christianity in the area, and blessings had followed heavily. He bought the farm, built the house and educated all his children, while expanding The Lord's reach to heathen souls that lay in sin, awaiting redemption.

The day ended swiftly and soon he found himself driving his Toyota Probox home. As usual, he dropped off some neighbours by the gate to his farm. Then he parked outside his bungalow and brought out a green bag that carried a half a kilogram of the liver delicacy his wife craved and a packet of sugar. The container with Triatix, his favourite acaricide for the cattle, he left in the storeroom before going into the house

"Ni wewe, ni wewe Bwana, ni wewe..." a song came to his lips. He quickly dropped off the green bag of provisions in the kitchen and declined a cup of tea until later.

Then he took his signature hat and walking stick and began his survey of the farm. His heart tickled with pleasure when he distinguished the lolling bell of his breeding bull in the herd, far away. He paused now and then to inspect fencing that had given way or a paddock that needed rest. He cursorily checked his herd of young calves and bulls and carefully inspected Maridadi, his lead bull, tethered by itself and satisfied himself the leash still held.

Only last month Maridadi had cut his tether due to urgent calls from a neighbour's cow. Maridadi's testosterone levels had dramatically exploded with this invitation, and he had mounted her so badly he had broken her back.

The Reverend tarried by the main herd as they humped home across the pastures, taking chunky bites of grass as they went. The herd leaders anxiously made for home while the laggards still grazed. He watched for animals that were not grazing, from practice; it was the first sign of disease. He was satisfied all was well.

Then for the last evening inspection, he made up his mind to check the progress of the work in the maize fields. Their golden hairs gently fluttered in the clammy evening air. He sank his gumboots into the soft, crunchy soil as he moved across the weeded portions. The air was hot and humid, and the long rains were nigh.

It was getting late. The sun was slowly dragging itself to the western horizon and it made grotesques patterns on the trees. He heard the thump! thump! thump! sound of furious weeding. He moved closer.

It was Mariamu, and she was clearing a clump of marigolds choking his young plants. He watched the rise and fall of her hoe as she worked. Then she rose to take a breather and he coughed.

"You startled me," she said, wiping her face on the hem of a handkerchief she had tied on her wrist.

"I was passing by and decided to check the weeding progress. Your hand is not bad...'" He waved his walking stick at the crest-fallen marigolds, brutally snuffed out and shaken to loosen the clump of soil on their roots, before Mariamu threw them on a pile like a pyre.

"Yes, I need to finish before the rains...." A hint of excitement was discernible in her voice as she talked to him. She then rose and looked at him, and for a moment they simply looked at each other.

His gaze lingered on her even when she turned away, embarrassed perhaps, and he noticed the slight dip of her dress on her backside as she wrapped a leso around her waist.

"It is late." He peered at the advancing veil of darkness.

"I am going now," she said, picking up her water-can. Then she moved over to a clump of maize stover, laid the hoe on the ground, and scooped some loose soil over it. Once it was fully concealed, she walked away.

"May it be well with you," she called out.

"May it be well with you too," he answered.

His eyes rested on her receding figure as she took a downward diversion to the lower fence and melted into the weak night light.

That is a temptation, an inner voice cautioned him. He suddenly felt exposed, and he realized what he felt towards her was attraction and not fear of being seen with her. He admitted to this as the normal attraction a man may feel towards a woman, but if it went too far, he thought, it became lust and sinful.

You want her... the devil prodded his conscience. He was sinking.

"Shetani ashindwe! Ashindwe kabisa," he rebuked the devil to reassure himself.

It is that old liar, he reckoned and felt reassured because he had fought the devil many times over the years and had come out unscathed over and over.

I will wake up to pray at midnight, he reassured himself, and he vowed to keep off the maize farm and let his wife oversee its progress.

He anxiously trudged homewards.

On the eastern horizon, the full moon rose grandly and bathed the land in soft, sensuous colours. Crickets urgently chirruped for their mates, while across the hedge, Maridadi mooed intermittently, pawed the ground in fury, and snorted. He then challenged the neighbouring bulls to a duel.

Nightfall came.

✝

The Reverend studiously avoided the maize field for the next few days. This was easy to achieve as he was away from home on Wednesday for a church fellowship across the ridge, and on the next two days, he applied himself at the shop and gave his assistant time off so he could expend his energy and have none to go surveying the farm when he got home. He hoped this would be enough time for Mariamu to complete work on the acre.

At idle times in the shop, he sat wondering why Mariamu unnerved him, after thirty years of service without blemish.

He had been an impressionable young man of twenty when he had met Reverend Livingstone. The Reverend had converted him, and he had felt the enormity of being born with the original Adamic sin. Once he was trained, he set out to proclaim the gospel, combing the district and winning converts, one by one.

There were epic battles over female circumcision and derision over marrying a meliaat, an uncircumcised girl, Rachel, his wife.

They met during a Church District congregational meeting, she a tall and graceful girl leading the Choir. She was from the neighbouring ridge. He had seen her in the local school before he'd moved to live with his uncle who was working in one of the tea estates in Kericho — to attend school there. Her towering frame captivated him, and he resolved to win her friendship. She was among a handful of pioneer school-going girls in the district. She became the talk of the entire community when she passed her K.A.P.E. exams and proceeded to do C.P.E. Thereafter she took a nurse aid course in the local Mission Hospital. By then, their romance was well on its way. They married shortly after her course.

God had been on his side as the sun set on the colonial adventure; he took advantage of his good reputation as a church leader to acquire prime farmland from the departing colonial settlers and switched over to modern living. Although the church did not pay him much as a part-time preacher, his farming enterprise paid off handsomely.

I have avoided temptation all along... Outside his shop, the town seemed to be evaporating in the sun

✝

The rains did not come. On Saturday evening, he was languorously taking a cup of tea at the shed under the bougainvillaea tree when Simba, his dog, pricked up its ears, and let out warning growls. Someone was coming.

Presently, a figure approached haltingly; it was a Chemosi, a casual farm worker. He quieted the dog.

After an exchange of pleasantries, the man explained that he need pay for work done that week. Rachel, who had assigned him the task, was not at home; she had gone for a Saturday prayer meeting. The Reverend felt he would rather not go to the farm to check the work, but the man insisted he needed his pay to buy foodstuff for his family.

He had to go.

They walked across the farm and in the late evening breeze, the maize plants flapped their leaves lightly, while in the distance, there were frenzied jerking motions among the plants, as if a witch were disturbing them underneath. Soft sound betrayed a worker at work as a hoe dug into the rich loamy soil.

He knew it was Mariamu.

Sweat beads decorated her face and her feet were bathed in brown dust. She smiled slightly, and he thought she gazed too invitingly at him. She then dipped downwards, and the green bustle swallowed her. The Reverend and the farmhand inspected the weeded sections. He paid the worker and the man departed.

He exited the maize farm and took an alternative route to the paddocks. In the fields, jutting out like little earth mounds, were his milking herd, reclining peacefully, after the evening meal of maize silage, its vinegary aroma lightly lingering in the troughs. His Nilotic heart glowed with pride, almost like a little boy who has a new toy and wakes up at night to confirm its presence. Then he went to the edge of the field and leaned on the wire fence and his practised eye searched for the heartthrob of his life, Maridadi, his breeding bull.

The bull's hulky frame was missing.

Where is Maridadi? he wondered. He must have cut his tether again and wandered into the neighbouring farm.

He stilled by a fence post to pick out distant sounds as he knew, from experience, he would hear Maridadi when the bull bawled a challenge to the other bulls.

Maybe I should call Albert to go for the bull, he thought. However, he made up his mind to round up the bull himself.

Presently, he picked up on Maridadi's call, and he knew the bull was down by the stream.

He was shooing the bull out of the stream when it wandered off into the thickets. He was so engrossed in his endeavours that he did not realize the bull had wandered into a section reserved for womenfolk to draw water and bathe.

He saw her then. There, ahead of him in a bend, was Mariamu covered in soapy suds. She had not seen him. His eyes lingered on her wet skin. He did not know how long he stood there before he understood he was committing a sacrilegious act.

He made to go and at that moment, Maridadi broke through a clump of gnarled leleshwa trees and made a dash for the deep end of the stream. She looked up, frightened.

Their eyes met.

He did not wait a moment longer. He scampered uphill and decided to pass by the workers' housing and instruct one of the herdsmen to go for the bull.

He needed not have worried, the bull soon made up its mind to re-join his harem. The Reverend found him trudging home to his herd like royalty, but the Reverend knew he would still have to call one of the herdsmen to get a fresh tether, failure to which the bull was likely to harass the milking herd the whole night.

"What a temptation. Shetani ashindwe!" he mumbled.

His mind was on fire as he thought of the buttery body he had just seen. He felt he needed to unburden his soul in prayer to ward off the devil whose presence he felt nearby, lurking like a hungry lion, ready to devour him.

He secluded himself on a rocky patch and strove to gather his scattered thoughts together. 'Lord! Lord...' he said. Then he lost his strength and he could not pray.

He stood to go and sensed someone was approaching. There, blocking his path, was Mariamu.

The devil... His mind raced.

"Mariamu..." he croaked.

"I came to pick my things." She pointed at the ground.

In the evening sun, he made out her water can and yellow carrier bag that carried isageek, a local vegetable.

He ran... but he was not fleeing. Instead, he was moving towards her, and he could smell the lemon fragrance of Geisha soap on her skin, and she was pulling him to herself, her supple arms encircling him, a faint smile, barely discernible on her face. They sought a grassy patch beneath a euphorbia tree.

†

Long afterwards, Rachel was shooing off Maridadi to his paddock. He had strayed and entered the banana groove in the main compound. Because it was Saturday, she knew the farmhands would have gone for a drinking bout without properly securing the livestock.

Presently, she stumbled on a water-can and yellow carrier bag. Besides them, was a walking stick and a flat cap.

What is happening? she thought, and her eyes scanned the horizon. She thought something twitched under the euphorbia tree.

On realizing what she was looking at, she felt a sudden, intense squeeze in her chest, as if an elephant were sitting on it.

Her knees wobbled and she fainted.

Kiprono Tonui studied Literature in English at the Kenyatta and Nairobi Universities. He previously worked as a high school teacher and part-time university lecturer. He has longed to be published; a dream realized in this anthology.

Mummy, Dearest

Olivia Kidula

Condom wrappers were intermittently strewn across the sand, and Adam watched in disgusted amusement as a large sand crab rushed by, a used condom glued to its leg, in hot pursuit. He gave a wide berth to a small group huddled suspiciously over a fire. As he approached the bar, he spotted a pallid-faced woman wearing a thin, black sweater with holes in the elbows, standing underneath a dying palm tree, hopping from one foot to another. Her eyes searched the beach with glaring intensity: someone needed to find her supplier soon. Already there was a man passed out by the stairs to the bar: spread-eagled, with his shrivelled penis peeking cheekily out of his shorts.

Sneering, Adam pushed the door open. A neon sign flickered weakly over the entrance – The Kingsborough, a highfalutin British name for a dive bar on the dirty coastal hems of Kenya. Of course, nobody ever called it that; it was Chill Ben's, after the owner. Adam flared his nostrils as he drew in the faint but distinct smell of damp cement, human perspiration, spilt beer, cheap cologne, tobacco, sodden wool and bile – a smell they never managed to wipe off the pleather seats or to ventilate.

"Smells just like home," he muttered. His urge to drink was overwhelming.

He always sat in the same spot, the stool farthest down the corner. When it wasn't occupied, that is, although it was nearly always empty. The bar was seldom crowded, and that particular seat was the most inconspicuous and the least comfortable. The speakers were shoved right in there as well, making the space even smaller, yet Adam preferred to spend most of his nights in that cramped space.

He spotted the proprietor hunched over the chipped and grimy bar top, having a not-so-chill discussion with one of the wait staff, who walked away muttering curses under his breath. Chill Ben launched into one of his usual tirades, this time directing bitter curses at whichever deity decreed that he should spend his years as a hotelier – part waiter and barman, all pimp. Still grumbling, he reached beneath the bar and pulled out a glass and an almost empty bottle of Konyagi, its contents still at the same level Adam had left it the night before. He made to pour Adam a glass but seeing the look on the young man's face, left the bottle on the bar top. Adam opened the cap and drank carelessly, alcohol spilling down his neck and onto the front of his shirt.

"Leo umeanza mapema," said Chill Ben.

Adam wiped his mouth and burped noisily in response.

According to Chill Ben, there were hundreds of different types of drinkers, but only two of those ever frequented his bar: those who drank to enhance lacklustre personalities, and those who sought to rid themselves of something. It was obvious to him that Adam belonged to the latter group, yet the old man could not tell what it was Adam was trying to be rid of. Perhaps a hereditary flaw, or trauma from his past, or perhaps something in the present was causing him problems. Maybe a combination of all those things. Chill Ben did not mind any type of drinker, as long as they never asked for credit and paid their tabs. Adam paid his in advance. This greatly pleased Chill Ben who had developed a soft spot for the young man. Whenever he found Adam in one of his rare good moods, he beckoned the young man to the back, where he had a simple table and two chairs. Under a cloak of incense, burning oil and songs that warbled in and out of a broken radio, they talked late into the night —the kind of conversations a parent has with his child when they had begun to grow bald together. Chill Ben brought out bottles far too pricey for the bar's usual clientele: rye bourbons and single malts. Adam detested whiskey — that was his mother's drink of choice — but he indulged Chill Ben, nodding in feigned approval when the older man gloated about the varying age and smoky tastes of each of the bottles in his prized collection.

Chill Ben guessed this was not to be one of those whiskey nights. He debated whether or not to pry, but instead opted to sit and observe Adam from his perch in the opposite corner of the bar.

✝

Something was shaking. At first, Adam thought it was an earthquake causing the flimsy foundations of the bar to shake. For a split second, he imagined the ground ripping apart, swallowing him, Chill Ben, his shitty bar and whiskey collection and the degenerates outside whole, and the ocean rushing in to bury them all. He put the Konyagi bottle down and delved into his pocket. His mobile phone vibrated in his hand. The display showed an unsaved number, but Adam knew exactly who it was calling for the umpteenth time today. He put the phone back in his pocket and avoided looking at his reflection staring back at him in the mirrored display behind the bar top.

"Was that Monica?" Chill Ben asked as he cleared the third empty bottle and deposited another one next to Adam. The bar owner regretted the question immediately; Adam tense up, a pained grimace on his face.

A feeling welled up in Adam's chest, nameless yet intimately familiar. A painful pressure rose to a crescendo behind his sternum, demanding release, like a wild creature trying desperately to claw its way out of his chest. He wished he could cut through his ribcage to free it. Instead, he reached for the new bottle in the manner zombies, barely hanging on to their half-deadness, reach for the neck of their next patsy.

He had been trying desperately not to think of her, yet he couldn't even be mad at Chill Ben's forwardness. The stench of sadness clung to him like a thick, smelly coat.

A nine-month-long bender of pills, psychedelics, and alcohol managed to muddle the exact details of how they were introduced or where they met, but he was unable to drown out the first moment he had seen Monica. He blushed at the memory of how badly he had wanted her. He had never experienced such overwhelming physical desire before; it was not the simple desire of someone wanting to pull her close, feel her lips and the soft heat of her body against his, but a brute dark forcefulness. He wanted to consume her, possess her in every sense of the word, feel what she was feeling, think what she was thinking. He wanted to feel a startling kind of intimacy with her, one that allowed him to experience her heartbeat as his own. With the estrangement and vagueness of recalling a dream, a series of blurred images flashed through his mind: his shock at her approaching him and asking to buy him a drink and feeling like an unsuspecting contestant on one of those unfunny prank shows; his incredulity growing as the night went on, as she laughed at his awkward jokes and said he was cute, and how he thought he might dissolve into a puddle when she asked him if he wanted to go back to her place; waiting for the camera crew to jump out of the bushes outside her apartment block; anticipating the choreographed peals of a studio audience mocking his naivete, a grinning game show host hopping out of the bathroom in her stead after she purportedly went to "freshen up".

But there was no surprise, it was all very real. She alone stood before him, in her lacy underwear. They spent every night together for a month before she asked him to move in.

Adam had felt unfamiliar happiness just being in her company, as though Monica had opened a secret door and beckoned him across the threshold — into a magical world of colour. Monica did that for him — she was his invitation to life, one he grasped with both hands.

So this is it, he thought. *This is love.*

He recognized it without question and knew clearly that he'd never experienced anything like it before. His previous romantic encounters had been brief and unsatisfactory for all concerned. He never seemed to find the special connection he longed for. He had believed he was too damaged, too incapable of intimacy. But every time he cracked a joke and heard Monica's contagious giggle, a wave of excitement ran through him. He loved to hear her talk even more. She made an art form of talking, balancing tones and verbs like a ballerina apportions her weight out on tiptoes. Through a kind of osmosis, he absorbed her youthful exuberance, her lack of self-consciousness and unbridled joy. He liked this new person, this unafraid man Monica inspired him to be. They fucked all the time. Adam was consumed with lust, perpetually, urgently hungry for her. He needed to keep touching her; he couldn't get close enough. When he proposed and she said yes, Adam wept.

Bizarrely, the first person he'd thought to tell was his mother. He wanted to introduce Monica to her, wanted her to see how happy he was, that he had finally escaped her, that he was free. In hindsight, it was a bad idea, doomed from the start, fatal hubris.

At the lunch, his mother at first seemed more depressed than usual. Quieter, smaller somehow, as if she wasn't there. Adam tried to fill the awkward silences with stories of his recent adventures with Monica and their future plans, but as he went on, she gave off a darker presence, increasingly unfriendly, glaring, unsmiling. She didn't take her cold, dark eyes off Monica the entire time. It was an uncomfortable lunch. She didn't seem to like Monica or feel particularly happy for them. He didn't know why he was surprised or why he felt guilt, a fist pressed to his chest.

When he and Monica left his mother's house, part of him didn't – forever a child, trapped.

The day after the visit, the phone calls started. She mostly called at the crack of dawn, making sure hers was the first voice he heard in the morning. He began to leave his phone charging in the next room as he slept, so his mother resorted to evening calls. The phone would ring around mealtimes, or just as they were retiring to bed. Long winding conversations about her imagined ailments and sexually inadequate ex-lovers.

The minute Monica raised an issue, Adam blocked his mother's number, and for a while, they were granted respite. Until his mother got her hands on Monica's personal line, then her office number, then started showing up at the office building, claiming Monica was keeping her child from her. Human Resources was not amused by the weekly semi-inebriated show, and neither was Monica. She told Adam quickly, perfunctorily, categorically that it was his duty to do whatever it took to fix his relationship with his mother and stop her from acting out. The 'or else' was implied. Terrified, he agreed to terms that satisfied both Monica and his mother: Adam would have to spend the night at his mother's twice a month. The phone calls and visits stopped, and everyone was happy. Except for Adam.

He thought that by letting his mother back into his life he would somehow fix the situation, but deep down he knew he was wrong, that it was all so wrong. He almost laughed out loud in Chill Ben's when his memory steered him back to his feeble attempt at rearranging the events of his childhood. When he tried to tell his mother that he would no longer be tolerating her behaviour, the tone of authority in his voice made him feel awkward, as if he were wearing clothes three sizes too big. Her response? "Don't be disgusting." Him! The disgusting one! A joke, if he ever heard one. Still, he felt the sting of her rejection all over his skin, as if someone had doused him with gasoline. It was too late, and it was all his fault – he had internalized his mother, let her shadow saturate his life and buried her deep down in his subconscious. He detested the fortnightly sleepovers, but they were so fundamental to his (but mostly Monica's) peace. He did not know how to even begin dissecting his mother's actions, let alone begin sharing them with his fiancée.

His thoughts careened towards what happened next, unstoppably, inevitably. There were gaps in those memories, a blurring where his blackouts slipped through and obscured his trauma, where reality distorted and bent. Still, disjointed flashes broke through the drunken fog.

The heavy feeling of dread came over him whenever he went to sleep in his childhood home, every surface in the house an exposed nerve; years of shame and guilt etched into the soul of the splintered hardwood, peeling paint and leaky roof. Bony fingers ripping the bedsheets away, revealing a bright harsh face bobbing above him. Her leso falling, exposing breasts that had collected in sagging puddles around her belly. The drive back to his house the next day, still sore and covered in a thick tar-like layer of disgust, the unsavouriness of the last few hours a palatable taste in his mouth. The intense misery he felt when he realized he was no longer able to have sex with Monica. The misery that burgeoned when she began to ask if it was her, if she had put on too much weight, if there was something she could do, if there was somebody else.

Her face unrecognizably contorted as she threw his phone at him, muscles pulling up and down in unexpected places, bawling something through downturned lips, of which he only caught "your own mother" and "fucking sick!" Him by her side patting her back in short awkward strokes, and her recoiling from his touch.

After she called off the engagement, he moved across the country, a drunken vagabond trying to escape his anguish, but no matter how far he ran, he carried both women with him wherever he went. Adam was pursued by an infernal, relentless chorus of Sirens — shrieking that he was worthless, shameful, a failure, that it was all his fault. He finally settled at the furthest tip of the coast, doing grunt work on a large fishing boat for next to nothing, just a place to stay and enough wages to keep him drowning in cheap gin.

✝

His phone's renewed vibrations restored the weft of reality. He brought it out again, intending to silence it, but instead accidentally opened the message display.

[26/03 16:39] I've missed my big strong man. When are you taking me on a date?

[26/03 16:42] Will you be in Nairobi over Easter? I bought you a gift for your birthday!

[26/03 16:45] Someone new moved in next door. I think ako campus. She has big tits vile tu unapenda ;)

[26/03 16:46] The creepy guy at work bought me lingerie o_O I tried it on anyway. I'm sending you a pic. Thoughts?

[26/03 16:47] lol.jpeg

Adam stood up abruptly and chugged the last of his drink. He said goodbye to Chill Ben and left the dive bar.

The crisp evening air should have been invigorating, but instead, it oppressed him. The half-naked man was no longer sprawled in front of the bar; as far as Adam could tell, the beach was deserted.

"Is that you?"

Adam turned. It was the junkie.

"It's you, isn't it? Have you come instead of Allano? I need a fix right away. I've-"

"Sorry," Adam interrupted. "I'm not who you think I am."

Leaning her head to one side, she narrowed her eyes, as though appraising whether he was lying to her. "No, seriously. I've seen you around here before."

"That doesn't make me a drug dealer."

"I know Allano doesn't want my stories because I haven't paid, but I promise I'll get you the money. I have this, it's very expensive!" She shoved a cold hard object into his hands. Adam looked at the hip flask that she had given him. It did look pricey; Adam guessed from the way the light bounced off the sleek exterior that it was made of platinum, but he couldn't be sure. His interest piqued when he heard liquid sloshing around the inside, but he recoiled in disgust when he twisted the cap and smelled whiskey.

"Look, I'm not Allano or whoever, but I have some. I'll give it to you, just so you leave me alone."

She paused, staring as if his words had to follow detours around scorched neurons and smashed synapses. Then the dull glow of understanding that Adam had anticipated lit up in her eyes.

She cocked her head, her thin anaemic lips tightening in anticipation. He reached into the side pocket of his shirt pocket and pulled out a tiny ziplock bag, trading it for the flask. Adam was not a fan of the brown stuff that was popular with the other beach bums; he had a bad trip the first time he had tried it and swore never again — but he carried the poison on him anyway, a bit like when the Nazis kept cyanide pills in the soles of their shoes. And now he tucked the whiskey flask into his shirt pocket.

She grinned at him gratefully, almost like she couldn't believe her luck. Because of her crooked chipped teeth, her smile did not seem so much childlike as canine, expressing all the guilelessness of a puppy wagging its tail.

She observed Adam, even in the pale moonlight she could see where vessels had burst under his skin, faded bruises that decorated his arms and knees. Something in his demeanour suggested to her that he had not been touched in a while, at least not without anger or fear or anxiety. His eyes were sunken and hollow, but they held a soul that rivalled star fire.

"Unakuwanga m-cute…"

"What?"

"Usijifanye huelewi." She held his eye. She gave him an obliging tilt of the head when he seemed to have understood. The crinkle of bafflement on his forehead rearranged itself into one of comprehension, his eyes did that quicksilver glint that betokened the immanence of speech, but no words came out. No words were needed anyway.

The vodka from Chill Ben's had yet to run its full course, so in his jumbled mind, the only reasonable thing to do was take her outstretched hand and follow her into the darkness.

†

Dilapidated buildings that used to be public restrooms stood beside rusty playground equipment a little away from the beach. A cottage necropolis marred the coastline like rotting teeth, littered with crushed cigarettes, dusty plastic bottles, a construction helmet, a dried bucket of paint, a white woman in a bikini on the cover of a crumpled magazine. The detritus followed them like an old conversation. Adam wasn't too familiar with the place, but the grim setting added a sordid, almost erotic appeal to the adventure.

They ducked into one of the abandoned rooms – it appeared to have been a storage area. Now nothing remained there, even the cobwebs bridging the blades of the ceiling fan had long been abandoned by spiders and conquered by dust. The floor was slick and sticky in places, gummy beneath his sandals. His foot crashed into a garbage bag, and the thin plastic split. His left foot sank into the moistness up to the shin, a sludge drowning his skin. The smell was unbearable. He looked at her apologetically, but she didn't seem to have noticed, and if she had, she didn't care. She lunged at him, prying his lips apart with her tongue. He stiffened at the abrupt move, and she might have sensed his discomfort because she softened and began kissing him with surprising tenderness. The taste of garbage remained in his mouth; acidic, like mould and rotten bananas. When he climaxed, his cum painted thick onto her exposed skin, a second layer of spoiled flesh.

After they were both dressed, she asked what his name was.

"Adam. What's yours?"

She told him.

"That's my mother's name."

"Is she a nice person?"

He laughed. "No, she's a whore, just like you."

She stared at him incredulously, and the look on her face made him laugh even harder. His maniacal laughter bounced off the walls of the tiny room and chased her as she ran towards the beach.

†

As the sun rose, he walked home, marching a familiar path through the loose sand and crumbling concrete. He had walked down the stretch of beach so many times, seen the stories of all those houses, staggered by as the sidings were pasted, the windows carefully installed, as some houses fell into disrepair and some fixed again, as apartment buildings were constructed and condemned and people moved in and out. His phone rang again. He reached into his pocket and threw it against a collapsing wall, where it broke into several pieces. Then from the other pocket, he produced the flask and drank deeply of the dirty, scorching whiskey.

Olivia Kidula is a writer and editor from Nairobi, Kenya. Her interests include photography, baking and pottery. Find more of her work on willthisbeaproblem.co.ke and her personal blog, dontcallmeliv.com

No Good Deed

Alvin Kathembe

I'm sitting at the bar on Saturday night, waiting for W__ and drinking a whiskey sour. This is the only place in Nairobi where they make them right, with the egg white and everything. The bartender knows me, and he always slips an extra tot into the cocktail. It comes with two little straws to drink out of – every time I take a sip, the alcohol hits my brain as through the barrels of a shotgun.

This place opened a couple of months ago and is only just beginning to pop. It's known well enough among the locals but is still too young to be the rage on Lonely Planet or TripAdvisor, so we're spared the influx of yuppie tourists and expats here to sample the 'Top 10 Nairobi Nightclubs You MUST Visit (No. 7 Will Surprise You!)'. We know it's just a matter of time, though: soon, the music will begin to change – subtly at first, perhaps beginning with dedicated 'Pangaea Nights' by imported DJs, or something of the sort, before going fully electronic. But we will still come. Then the bouncers will begin to speak in English and will let us in only after a minute inspection of our IDs, an extremely invasive pat-down and a disdainful scowl, as other patrons of exalted station (and complexion) waltz past. But we will still come. Finally, the price of drinks will double, and that is the only way they will get rid of us.

This is my third whiskey sour and I'm floating in that blissful middle-ground between tipsy and reckless. W__ was supposed to meet me here at ten. I can always approximate the time, on a night out, just going by the music. Between sunset and eleven p.m., they play old-school jams as they try to lure people in – Nelly and Kelly's 'Dilemma'; some Nameless; some Tupac; some E-Sir. Then between eleven and three a.m., the DJ turns up the tempo with whatever's the rage of the month — Nigerian or Bongo music or the latest local hits — as people get ratchet on the dancefloor. Past that, the music slows to dirge-like R&B ballads; the perfect soundtrack to drunken regret, loneliness, and last-ditch long shots. Right now, the DJ's playing Ethic's 'Figa', and W__ is late.

I finish my drink, and I'm about to turn to the bartender for another when I feel a tap on my shoulder.

"Hey, weirdo, why are you drinking by yourself?"

W__ and I have known each other since we were toddlers growing up in the same housing estate in Donholm. She moved away when I was 13, but we kept in touch: we wrote each other letters in high school and texted through flip phones stolen from older siblings. We chatted on 2go about the latest MP3s and games we'd downloaded off Waptrick. We were close all through college – she studied Law at the University of Nairobi while I studied Engineering at JKUAT. Today, she runs her own business selling clothes on Instagram, and I work in the HR department at my uncle's firm.

She tells me about her day, a funny story about her Uber driver, and updates me on how her business is doing. I make little noises to move the conversation along as I signalled the bartender to fix us some more drinks.

"…anyway, after last weekend — it was madness, I tell you, absolute chaos — I made three resolutions that I'll never, ever break." She pauses for a bit, to sip from her Long Island and to invite me, eyes twinkling, to ask.

"What resolutions?"

"I'm never going out with M__ again! She is crazy, out of her mind, and quite frankly dangerous. I want nothing to do with her."

I laugh and put the barrels to my mouth again. Boom. "And the second?"

"I'm never doing acid again!"

"You're crazy, you know that?"

"It was a terrible idea. I was already drunk out of my mind by the time M__ brought the blotters out. It felt like reality was broken – like I was watching a movie with really badly done special effects. I was laughing like a crazy person, going around pointing at things, saying crazy stuff like 'y'all expect me to believe this?' It was awful."

W__ illustrates her stories with exaggerated gestures, throwing her hands around carelessly. People around her are as likely to find themselves doubled over from a blow as from laughter. Just now she has almost knocked the tray from the hands of a passing waiter. He shoots her a dirty look – she doesn't even notice.

"I wish I was there to see that!" I say, still laughing. "This M__ sounds like quite the character, I should meet her."

"She's coming in a bit, I told her to meet me here."

"But you just said…"

"My third resolution," she cuts in, ignoring me, "is this: the next time I go out with M__, and she offers me some acid, I'll only take half."

I just shake my head. She downs the rest of her drink in one big gulp, then points toward the entrance.

"There she is now. Over here!"

M__ is wearing a stylish low-cut red blouse and black jeans. She sees W__ waving and makes her way over.

After a hug and extended greeting, W__ gestures toward me. "This is Leo: Leo, M__."

"Hi," she says, offering her hand, and I shake it. Her nails are short and painted beige. She wears a gold ring on the forefinger of her left hand to go with the gold watch on her wrist. On her right finger, she wears a bracelet beaded in the colours of the Kenyan flag. Her hands are soft. Her face is smooth, and glowing somehow, as if from a radiance within her. It looks moist, like if I touch it, my hand will come away with a smudge of chocolate.

Her eyes are brown, or black — I feel like I could stare into them for hours, trying to figure her out. Right now, they are looking at me, twinkling half in challenge, half in interest. I read somewhere that the real reveal of character is not the eyes, however; eyes have their secrets, and hers hide them well. The real tell is the mouth. The lips, really. All the subtler hints of human character are written in those little slivers of skin if one knows how to read them: greed, arrogance, cruelty, resolve. She has full, impudent lips that flux easily into a playful smile. She is not wearing lipstick. Her lower lip has a little protuberant patch of skin in the centre of it. She licks this lower lip, running the tip of her tongue across the top of it. This might be just a thing that she does unconsciously, or maybe she does it for me to see. Whatever the case, I see it, and from the way her cheeks flush slightly, and from the tiny, sudden tension in the corner of her mouth, I know that she has seen me see it.

"…she's a journalist, she writes for 'Mkenya'. Leo's got a cushy job at his rich uncle's company," W__ is saying, with a smirk.

"What do you do for your rich uncle?" M__ teases, eyebrows arched.

"HR stuff. Hiring and firing messengers, that sort of thing." I reply. Maybe a little too bitterly? "Great use of my Geospatial Eng. degree – well-spent five years on that," I add, for levity, and we all laugh.

"Yeah, I did IT in uni," M__ says. The bartender brings around six tequilas. "Here's to useless degrees!" I say.

The night melts into a warm, comfortable rhythm of good music and easy conversation. M__ and I exchange playful banter, lobbing harmless jokes at each other. When W__ announces that she needs to go to the bathroom, M__ offers to accompany her, and I make a joke about how dangerous women's bathrooms must be, seeing as one can never risk it alone.

"We're going to gossip about you, dummy," W__ says, sticking her tongue out.

Everyone keeps asking why W__ and I have never had a thing. They point out that we have great chemistry and are always hanging out together. I never seem to be able to explain our relationship and why it'll never be a romance. The idea itself is offensive, maybe even a little incestuous. I dated her best friend once. She dated my cousin. Both ended badly, and we vowed to never fix each other up again. I signal to the bartender for another round of shots, and by the time he's poured them, the girls are back.

"So, what did she tell you about me?" I ask M__, when she's back on the barstool.

"I told her the truth," W__ cuts in.

I let out a mock-groan. "You're supposed to be my friend!"

M__ laughs. "To friendship," she says, raising her shot glass, and we all share in the toast.

"Guys, I have a joke," I say. M__ looks at me expectantly, W__ groans and rolls her eyes.

"What do they call it, in Jamaica, when you spill your drink?"

"What?" M__ asks.

"Dutty wine."

W__ snorts into her drink. M__ laughs and smacks my arm playfully.

"That was a good one!" I protest.

"It was criminal." W__ scoffs.

"What's criminal is that jacket you're wearing," M__ says, pointing at me.

"Oof, buuurn!" W__ hoots.

I'm wearing a camouflage-print bomber jacket. It's warm and pretty cool, I think. It's a cold July night.

"What's wrong with my jacket?"

"Haven't you heard? The National Police Service sent out a tweet saying cops will arrest any civilians 'donning attire resembling police or military uniforms.' Apparently, you guys are creating confusion among the public."

"How do you know I'm not a cop?" I ask.

"You're the HR guy," M__ says, rolling her eyes.

"Sure, but I know how to use handcuffs, and I've been told I have an arresting personality."

That earns me another laugh. This time M__'s hand lingers a microsecond longer than necessary on my arm.

"Jokes aside, I saw that 'Hessy wa Dandora' guy threatening people on Facebook," M__ says. "Just be careful. I covered four shootings of unarmed, innocent young men just last week."

W__ snorts. "I'm sure those guys were far from innocent."

"They at least deserved their day in court," M__ says, frowning. "Do you honestly support cops having the licence to kill like that?"

"In some cases. The police know who these guys are, some are really rotten apples."

"Everyone is innocent until proven guilty. Leo could be in danger just for wearing this jacket, does he deserve to be gunned down with no due process? People are being killed out there."

"You know the kind of guys I'm talking about, not people like us," says W__. "Anyway, this conversation is killing my vibe, let's have some more shots!"

M__ sighs. Her bag is vibrating, she reaches in and pulls out her phone. "I have to leave, Ben is here."

"Ben?" I ask.

"Yes, my – my boyfriend," she says, almost apologetically. She catches my eye and blushes a little.

"I don't like him. I keep telling you: that guy is trash," W__ says, folding her arms.

M__ shrugs. "He knows you don't like him, that's why he's waiting for me in the car outside."

M__ gets up to leave. W__ rises with her. "I'll walk you to the car," she says.

"You just want to stir up some shit, eh? I know you!" M__ shakes her head, smiling.

I say a reluctant goodbye and get up to hug her. As I lean in, she runs her hands up my chest and over my shoulders — very subtly, and quickly, so no-one else notices — then up around my neck as she pulls her body against mine. I catch the faintest whiff of perfume; something heavy, something musky. Something that lingers.

"You smell nice," she says. I try to reply, to say something memorable, but all the blood seems to have rushed from my brain and gone somewhere else.

W__, who has been watching all the while, laughs, winks at me, then grabs M__'s arm and out they go. At the exit, just before she disappears, M__ turns back for one last look. Our eyes lock, and in that moment, I know — we both know — what will happen, eventually, and all the boyfriends in the world can't stop it.

When W__ comes back, she sits on the barstool beside me.

"Stay away from her," she says, "she's one of the good ones."

"So am I. I'm your friend, you should want the best for me."

"I'm trying to protect you both, from each other."

"I can handle myself. So can she."

"She has a boyfriend."

"Just the one."

W__ laughs and shakes her head. "Whatever. Don't say I didn't warn you."

"I feel like we really hit it off. She's interesting."

"Pfft, she flirts with everyone."

I laugh. "Maybe, but I really felt a spark."

"That's what they all say."

I shrug. "Still, thanks for introducing us."

W__ frowns. "I have a feeling I'll end up having to patch up both your sorry hearts when all this is over!"

"You know what they say – no good deed..."

We sit at the bar for a while, in companionable silence. W__ orders another round and downs her cocktail.

"Wow, take it easy!"

"Another one," she slurs. The bartender looks at me. I shrug, and he begins to mix.

"I shouldn't have taken that pill," she groans.

"What pill?" I ask, alarmed.

"In the bathroom. I told you that girl is bad news."

"Ah, shit. OK, that's it, no more for you." I take the glass from her and pour her drink into a nearby potted plant. The bartender glowers at me.

The DJ's playing Joe's 'I'm Missing You'. Bodies are strewn all around us, the flotsam of a Saturday night: there's a guy slumped over the bar beside us, snoring; three girls stagger past us, two of them half-carrying, half-dragging the third between them, and there's a yellow patch of vomit down the front of her blue dress. I ask for the bill.

When it comes, I take one look and my eyes water. Wueh!

"Boss, kwani how much is a Long Island?"

"Eight-fifty."

"Ai, how? Si last weekend I was here? They were only seven sock then!" I protest, a little too loudly. I sense movement behind me, a hovering by my elbow.

"We adjusted our prices." The bartender says, with a shrug.

"Is there a problem, sir?" the bouncer asks.

I check my MPESA balance. I'm short by 400/-. I look over at W__: she's staring at her hand like she has never seen it before. She wags her fingers, then laughs excitedly. Shit. Fuliza will have to cover the deficit.

"No problem," I mumble, looking up for the bar's paybill number.

†

I'm parked outside W__'s place, planning my route home. She lives in Kabete, so there was little risk driving from Westlands to her place. The way home from here is a little trickier: the night is dark and full of terror, and Alcoblow. I pull up my Google Maps and scan the routes. Little red lines of congestion, at 3 a.m. on Sunday morning? That could only be a police roadblock. I map out a less direct route through several backroads and set off.

I roll my windows all the way down, and the fresh air helps to clear my head. I put on some music – Sage's 'Maskini'. I drive at a steady 60kph. I slide down Waiyaki Way onto Uhuru Highway, down past the University Way and Kenyatta Avenue roundabouts. At the Haile Selassie roundabout, I turn right, into Upper Hill. I manoeuvre onto Bunyala Road and down toward South B. There they are, just as I expected, on the stretch of Uhuru Highway between the Bunyala Road and Haile Selassie roundabouts. I slow down to watch. One man has tried to run over the roadblock, and now the spike strip is lodged in the front bumper of his Probox. The policemen are trying to remove him from his car. He slides over to the passenger seat, opens the door, and makes a run for it – the cops scurry after him. He is incredibly fast; he streaks across the tarmac like a rat on the highway. I drive on.

I'm almost past Mater Hospital now. I'm thinking of M__, her red top and brown eyes. Her lips. I'm thinking of how she felt pressed against me like that, of that last lingering look we'd shared. I cringe when I remember how tongue-tied I'd become, how I'd fluffed that goodbye. I can still smell her scent on my jacket: hope, danger, recklessness, and a hint of musk. Then I see him.

He's lying under a streetlamp, right opposite the hospital, just sprawled on the concrete sidewalk. I slow down further and look at him as I drive past.

I don't know why: maybe it's the cold, or just me sobering up, but he makes me think of that boy, from all those years ago. I was fifteen, maybe sixteen. It was after dark, around seven p.m., and I was walking past Ambassadeur Hotel in downtown Nairobi, on the way to the stage to catch a matatu home. It was cold. I was wearing my new hoodie. It had cost me three thousand bob, and to my sixteen-year-old self that was a small fortune. It was black and had a picture of Lil' Wayne on it, with the caption 'BEST RAPPER ALIVE.' All my friends admired and envied me for it, and I felt like the coolest kid in the world.

A boy my age or younger was lying huddled in one of the traffic islands on the road outside the hotel. He was curled up into a ball, and he was cold. God, how he was shivering. I remember feeling so sorry for him. I wondered if he was sick — he must have been, I've never seen someone tremble like that. Come to think of it, he might have been having a convulsion of some kind. I remember thinking, *I wish I could help this kid, I wish I could give him a warm bed, or a hot meal. Take him to a doctor.* But I couldn't, I was sixteen years old with fifty bob in my pocket. I remember thinking that I should at least give him my hoodie — he had nothing but a ragged T-shirt on. But my hoodie was very nice, and I'd saved for so long to buy it. I doubt that there was anything that I could have done to help that poor kid, but right now, remembering, I feel… something. Uncomfortable.

I make an illegal U-turn right there on the road. I drive back, past where the man is lying, and make another illegal U-turn, and stop a few meters behind him. I stuff a two-hundred-shilling note into the inside pocket of my nice bomber jacket. I jump out of the car and walk, warily, to where he's lying. I stop a meter away. Is he dead? No, I can hear him breathing wheezily. I go closer. I know this guy, he hangs around the shopping centre, engaging in good-natured ribbing with the shopkeepers; trying to cajole a few shillings out of passers-by through flattery, or by offering to wash their cars. Just the harmless neighbourhood drunk, the kind of guy everyone in the hood knows by sight. He's holding a bottle of Kenya Cane in the crook of his armpit: the stench of alcohol is almost overpowering. I cover him, carefully, with the jacket and jog back to my car.

I drive the rest of the way home feeling like someone has lit a small fire in my chest. I decide that this is something I will keep to myself, a moment I will cherish as mine, and mine alone. I park, with a little difficulty, and salute my sleepy watchman as I race up the stairs to my apartment. I kick off my jeans, collapse into bed, then sleep the dreamless sleep of the righteous.

†

It is seven-thirty p.m. on Sunday evening, and I'm back at the same bar. This time I'm seated on one of the tables facing the giant canvas screen they project football games on. The table is littered with beer bottles and the debris of four or five whiskey sours. W__ is here, Tom is here, Mike is here, Mwangi is here; and drinks are on me, because I am suddenly and improbably rich.

This is what happened: I've been here since three-thirty. I had exactly two hundred bob in my wallet, and a Fuliza deficit of 400/- from last night. Challenge accepted. I pulled off a feat of financial legerdemain that I'll be bragging about all week. My two most pressing problems were both mobile money loans: 6000/- from M-Deni due today, and 7000/- on M-Shwari, due tomorrow. Both apps had been spamming me with increasingly aggressive reminders. I tried to borrow the money to pay these off from the other loan apps I have installed on my phone, but I'm maxed out on all of them. So I called Tom, who owed me 6000/-, and coaxed/threatened him into paying me. Once he agreed to pay up, I jokingly suggested he loan me an additional 2000/- which I'd pay back with 50% interest at the end of the month. Stunningly, he agreed, and my phone dinged with a message confirming my good fortune.

After Fuliza took its 400/-, I had 7600/- to work with. Then I called my sister. I gave her a sob story about how hard this month had been on me, and could I borrow 6k until payday? Boom. M-Pesa balance: 13,600/-.

I paid my M-Deni loan, and I had 7,600/- left. I had two choices. I could pay off my M-Shwari, take the remaining 600/-, drink my two beers and go home. That would have been the responsible thing to do. Did I do that? No. If I had done that, I would not be sitting here right now, like a king, with all my friends drinking on my tab, and a bottle of Jameson on the way. It was almost five p.m. when I paid up at M-Deni. The afternoon premier league games were just about to kick off. I pulled up my favourite betting app and checked today's odds. I transferred 7k to my betting purse, made my bets, and ordered those two beers. I won 15k and called the whole crew to come help me celebrate.

My original plan was to spend 5k or so, then pay off my M-Shwari debt with the rest. Then I heard W__ on the phone talking to M__, telling her where we were and asking her to come, so I ordered the bottle of Jameson. Life is for the living; tomorrow will take care of itself.

"Ay boss, I hear you've ordered a boti," Tom says, loudly. Everything about him is loud: his voice, his shirt, everything. "Si I holla at some mamis they come through?"

W__ rolls her eyes. "Tom," she says sweetly, "how come you never invite your 'mamis' over when it's you paying the bill?"

"Heh, look at this one now," Tom says, staring daggers at her. They hate each other, always have.

"Just saying," W__ says, staring right back.

"I host my friends all the time. When I do, I take care of everything. You hear me? E-ver-y-thing."

"I've literally never seen you do this," W__ says with a bemused smirk.

"You wouldn't, because when I host my friends, you're not invited."

"OK, OK," Mike cuts in, "that's enough."

Tom walks off to make his phone calls, and W__ is seething.

"I don't understand why you hang out with that guy," she says. "He's just a fucking leech."

"He's my friend," I say.

"He's a leech," W__ insists. "That's the kind of 'friend' you don't need."

"But us dudes are not like you," Mwangi says. "You chicks are cold. You could be friends with a girl for twenty years, then one day out of the blue you decide she looked at you funny, and just like that, she's cut off."

Mike laughs. "Us guys are different," he says. "A dude sits next to you in class two, and your friends forever. Twenty years later, he's the biggest asshole — you know, that guy at the party who's rude to your girlfriend and hits on your sister. We'll just laugh and be like, 'anakuwanga tu hivo.'"

"Anyway. I've said my piece." W__ sighs. "Speaking of which, I didn't mean to stick you with the bill last night, Leo. I was just super high. How much do I owe you?"

"Don't worry about it."

Mwangi groans at the screen and swears loudly. "I can't believe it, we're already one-nil down then they go and give away a penalty! We can't lose this game!"

"LOL," W__ says, and no, she doesn't laugh out loud: she actually says 'lol', as if it's a real word. "Dude, it's Arsenal, that's what you do."

An argument ensues, and I almost join in, then out of the corner of my eye, I see her.

Today she's wearing a white top and blue jeans. She's let her hair down, and I notice that there are little golden beads woven into the extensions. She looks a bit tired, like she's had a long day, but her eyes light up when she sees me, and my heart jumps. I get up to greet her.

"Hi," she murmurs. We hug, and there's that scent again — musky, risky.

"Heeeelllloooo, who is this?" Mwangi has stood up and is ogling M__. He doesn't even notice when Crystal Palace score the penalty and his beloved Gunners go 2-0 down.

"Everyone, calm down," W__ says, laughing. Introductions are made all round, and M__ takes the seat I strategically saved for her, between me and W__.

"How are you?" I ask.

"Tired," she replies. "I've had quite the day."

"Pole," I say. "Drink?"

"Yes please."

Tom comes back, and two girls are with him. They're both dressed in expensive but slightly garish outfits, their faces flawless, mask-like. They greet us with an aloof coolness, and size us up quickly. I look decent, since I suspected (and hoped) that I might meet M__ today. Mike always looks good: jeans, white shirt, black jacket. We're greeted civilly enough. Mwangi's wearing dirty blue jeans and a tired old Arsenal jersey. Like, really old, the ones with 'O2' on the front, 'Henry, 14' on the back. He gets a sneer, a fleeting fingertip handshake and a look that says 'you, sir, have been weighed on the scales and been found wanting.' Tom shouts for extra chairs, and they sit. When my Jameson comes around, he immediately takes possession of it, 'blesses' it, and proceeds to pour us drinks, beginning with his two friends.

"Na Coke iko wapi? Na ice? Ebu leta glasses zingine tatu. Harakisha bana!"

I sneak a look at W__: she is livid.

I turn back to M__. "Did Ben drop you off?" I tease, and she sighs.

"We had the biggest fight this morning. I got called to cover a story, but he wanted me to go hang out with his boys, eat nyama and whatever else," she says, shaking her head. "He got so mad when I told him I had to go to work."

"Sounds like he's a bit of an ass."

"You're biased."

"I'm not, I've never even met the guy. I'm just analysing the facts dispassionately."

She laughs, and some of the weariness fades from her face. She might just be the loveliest thing I've ever seen.

"Was it a very bad fight?" I ask.

"Yes." She frowns. "I think that's it for us."

"The end of love. A tragedy."

She smiles. "I don't think I'd use the word 'love' to describe our relationship."

"Well, if you need a shoulder to cry on, I'm here."

She laughs, rests her head on my shoulder, and closes her eyes.

"Hey, what's going on over there?" W__ shouts. I shoot her a dirty look, that cockblocking agent of Satan.

"I'm tired," M__ says, without opening her eyes. "I got called to work today."

"What was the assignment?"

M__ frowns and sits up. "Actually, it's about an extra-judicial killing. It's so weird, we were talking about this just yesterday."

"What happened?" I ask.

"We were called by this activist, his name is Jakim Mbogo."

"I follow him on Twitter," I say.

"Yeah, so he calls and says this guy has been gunned down in South B, and he needs some cover on it."

"In South B? That's my hood."

"Really? Did you hear anything?"

"Nothing. Where in South B?"

"Around Mater hospital," M__ says. "Anyway, this guy was shot, and the cops have refused to release the body to his family or even give any information regarding the shooting."

"Around Mater Hospital?" I repeat, slowly.

"Yes, she said that already," W__ cuts in. "So why was the guy shot?"

"The cops would only say that they recovered police paraphernalia, stolen money, an illegal firearm, and five rounds of ammunition."

"They were justified, then," W__ says.

"That's just the thing. The gun might have been planted on him. Apparently, the money recovered was less than five hundred bob. We found witnesses who said that his only crime was trying to run away when the police approached him."

W__ shrugs. "So you were there the whole day?"

"Yep, the whole day. So draining."

"Well you're here now, have a drink, unwind." W__ says. "After this, I'm thinking we go back to Leo's and play some board games, watch movies, maybe smoke a blunt..."

M__ smiles. "Sounds good. I can't stay too late though, tomorrow's Monday."

"Sure," W__ says. "Leo don't say I never did anything for you, eh?" she winks and digs an elbow into my ribs.

"Leo, are you all right?" M__ asks. My head is swimming.

"Leo, what's up?"

"Leo? Leo—"

"I—I need to leave," I manage to say, finally. Everyone stops talking and looks at me.

"Bro, are you OK?" Mwangi asks, concerned.

W__ springs into action. "Come on, Leo, let's get you some air."

She takes my hand and leads me out of the bar to my car. She takes the keys from me and unlocks it. She guides me into the passenger seat, then sidles round into the driver's and closes the door.

"What's wrong?" she asks after we've sat in silence for a while.

I try to answer, but there is a lump of emotion caught in my throat, choking me, drowning my words.

"It's ok, it's ok," she says. "Breathe. Just breathe. I'm going to take you home, ok? Whatever it is, we'll figure it out. Just hang in there."

She starts the engine and begins to back out of the parking lot. Her phone rings, and she stops the car to answer.

"Hello, M__? Yes, we're leaving, Leo's not feeling well. Yes, right now. Should you what? I can't hear you, it's too—oh, you want to come?"

She looks over at me.

"No, not tonight," she says. "Maybe some other time."

Alvin Kathembe is also a poet. His work has appeared in Omenana, The Short Story Foundation Journal, Brittlepaper, and other publications. Find him on Twitter as @SofaPhilosopher

Our Husband

Awuor Mugeni

After Mama met John, she asked me if I loved him. I said I wasn't sure.

"Good," she replied. "You should marry him."

Had I known any better, I wouldn't have listened to her. I would have run into the arms of Don, the man who actually loved me. But we are our parents' children, and in my Mama's house, comfort and security came before trivial things like romantic love.

Baba had given us the perfect example years before, by running off to be with a woman who had produced for him a son with a big forehead like his. Mama had begged him to stay because she loved him. She had even gone to see our Shosho, to beg her to convince him. But our uncles had turned her away, with permission from their mother, and ridiculed Mama for birthing only girls. She came home that day looking beaten and defeated and remained so for many months. I didn't go to school that year, although I was meant to have enrolled in the first year of secondary school, but after Mama got over her grief, she made sure that none of us was ever sent home again because of school fees. And no boy was ever welcome in our tiny compound.

I knew I had to have John the moment I saw him at a church event. He had a girlfriend then. A small, shy girl who led the choir with more spirit than she displayed in everyday life. I befriended the girl, and in a few months, made John want to have me around him all the time. They broke up, and the girl moved to another church.

John courted me with the zeal of David pursuing Bathsheba. His texts would have made King Solomon blush. And I would have given him the twitter award for best boyfriend ever, had I not despised people who performed their relationships on social media. Wherever we went, whether the club or the church, women either commented that we were perfectly matched, or whispered behind my back that I was not worthy of him. Who cared? I was happy in every sense of the word, except one. For someone who seemed so worldly, who said he went to church only because his parents had instilled a sense of religiosity in him, John strongly believed that we should not have sex before marriage. I wasn't a slut or anything, but no sex after dating for a whole month? And this went on for the whole year we dated.

But I stayed with him because getting married to John promised significant benefits. Mama's favourite was the allowance she received from him every month, which she liked to call her salary. John also made sure my younger sisters, in USIU and Strathmore respectively, never lacked for anything. I was the best-dressed woman in Nairobi, and True Love magazine wanted to feature our house. My favourite benefit, however, was quitting my job to be a stay-at-home wife, whose sole purpose in life was to spend John's money as I saw fit. I also got to sometimes flirt with his best friend,

Wicky, whose texts read eerily like the ones John had sent me while we were courting.

The downside of our union was that John seemed to not like me very much after we wed. We still had our conversations, and he treated me like a good friend, and most days, like his sister. The sister he used to say he wished he had. So Wicky became the man John was supposed to be as my husband. Our innocent flirtations turned into passionate trysts in my guest bedroom, whenever John was away on long business trips. John and I attempted to have sex twice after the wedding, and each session ended in frustration and humiliation for both us. John seemed unable to get it up for me. I thought it was a medical problem, but he insisted it was not and must have been something he had eaten or drank. But he started avoiding me, and I started doing everything to please him. I cooked all his favourite meals. I came up with activities and outings that I thought he would enjoy. I dressed impeccably to show off my curves and booty. I bought lingerie and toys, but only once did he show the tiniest interest, when I mentioned getting porn. He stared at me for about ten minutes straight, and I was afraid he was going to pour holy water on me.

It wouldn't have been so bad if I were the only one who craved having a baby, but my mother-in-law, Mrs. Mwamba was incessant about an heir. The conversation about children came up every time senior Mrs. Mwamba and I were together. Over tea, at the golf club, in the supermarket, if she ran into me visiting John at their insurance company, at church, inside every room in our five-bedroomed house and once, she sent me a maternity care kit. Finally, she recommended that I see a gynaecologist. A friend of hers, who was reputed to be very good, money be damned.

John sighed and sighed when I told him I'd made an appointment with the gynae. He walked up and down the length of our large living room, then said okay, and took his handsome face elsewhere, without saying anything else. But he didn't show up for that appointment, or the one I rescheduled after that, or even the next one. Finally, I decided to go alone. The gynae did some tests then advised me to come back with my husband after a week. I told John about it, texted him and included it in his calendar, even went as far as asking Jojo, his executive assistant, to turn down any meeting requests for him on that particular day, but he didn't show up. I vaguely remember breaking some Crystal glasses his mum gave us for a wedding present because two nights before the appointment, John didn't come home, and I didn't see him until the day after the appointment.

I was sure the gynae was updating my mother-in-law but thought that if Mrs. Mwamba saw how much effort I was making, she would convince her son to change for my sake. Somehow, I had learned to love John. I didn't understand his ways, but he did so much for me, and willingly. When I complained, Wicky told me that was just how John was. Unpredictable. Emo.

"Women are not his thing. Golf, business deals, cars, maybe." Wicky said to me one day, when I asked him if John might be seeing someone else. "He also hates doctors and hospitals," he added. 'But I can go with you to the gynae... It will be just like when we were planning 'our' wedding, eh?" He laughed.

I pulled a face and smacked him on the head.

Wicky had been with me at every step of the wedding planning. Where John refused to show up or participate, Wicky magically filled his shoes. He had famously helped me wrangle my mother-in-law into accepting my choice of flowers for the church and reception, and he even agreed to pay for the very expensive tulips: called it my wedding present. Senior Mrs. Mwamba had to donate her roses elsewhere.

I turned Wicky down on accompanying me to the gynae. I wanted John there and badly.

But it was a good thing John didn't come, because my test results came back positive for pregnancy. I was five weeks along.

Wicky wasn't picking up his phone. My mind seemed to have turned into coagulated milk. I went and sat inside the Range Rover, a one-year anniversary gift from John. I called the office and asked for John. He was out, they said. I called Jojo, but she wasn't picking up her phone either.

I drove from Parklands towards home in Westlands in a haze. It was slow, but I appreciated the traffic jam for the first time in my life. I hadn't had to think this hard since I left my marketing job at an Ad agency. There was hardly any hope of passing the child off as John's, even if I managed to get him into bed that same day. Wicky was dark where John was yellow-yellow like mustard. The child could take my milk chocolate tone, but John would very likely still know. Then, I would have to start tarmacking for a job. But I wasn't ready to go back to the corporate world. In as much as I said I'd quit to grow my family, I'd really just been tired of the bullshit. I really did love watching 'Keeping Up with the Kardashians' all day and catching up with the gossip on 'Kilimani Mums, Uncensored'. And shopping without worry about cash. And what was better than daytime drinking? I bit my lip at what would happen to my sisters. God forbid they had to transfer to the University of Nairobi: Mama would never stop blaming me for messing up their chances.

I sensed a migraine gathering in the far corners of my mind, which made me realise I was hungry. I could picture a burger with the intensity of a 3D Imax show and knew the craving was not going to go away now that I was pregnant.

An extremely loud hoot annoyed me out of my thoughts. A colourful matatu was behind me, and the makanga had come over to my window to check if there was a problem.

'Amka Msupaa!' he shouted. 'Tuko biashara, mamaaa!"

There were no longer any cars ahead of me; I was holding up traffic.

Feeling flustered, I opted to go into the Java restaurant I spied ahead. It was lunchtime, and the restaurant was packed to the brim. I figured I might as well order takeaway and eat in the car since I was in no mood to share tables with strangers.

As I strolled towards the counter, I noticed a lady with beautiful, voluminous, black hair – a Brazilian weave worth 100K at least. I couldn't see her face, but I could see who she was lunching with. The handsome man resembled John, but with the shadow of a beard.

I startled. It was John. He seemed engrossed in a very intimate conversation with the woman. Her hair and his clean-shaven head almost touched. Their food was mostly uneaten, and his right hand and her left hand sat very close to each other on the table. Thick as thieves, those two. Must be the reason why he can't get it up for me, I thought. Feeling faint, and fearing they would spot me, I stepped back out of the restaurant then peeped inside just as the woman turned her head to look for a waitress. That was Jojo's unmistakable profile. An entire bucket of acid flooded my stomach, melting my insides. They had been together all this time?

"Excuse me," said a customer trying to go past, out the restaurant's narrow doorway. I pulled back to give him the way. Several people walked in as I just stood there. John's infectious laughter lifted me out of the abyss I was sinking into, and I remembered to turn away just as he followed Jojo out of the restaurant. I squeezed behind the restaurant's door like a rat and turned my face to the wall. When I looked up, they had both disappeared among the parked vehicles.

I didn't feel very hungry after all, but I had a burning thirst for alcohol. So, I went back into my Range and drove around the corner to Brew Bistro. Then I called Jojo and asked her to meet me there. She arrived a few hours later and immediately ordered a Nyatipa. I had already had several whiskey sours by then and was burning to confess to her that I was pregnant with her boyfriend's child. We had never been friends, despite her being Wicky's girlfriend and constantly in John's vicinity – doing her job, or so I thought until earlier that day. She was so different from me, with an especially bad sense of style, I had never even thought to suspect her as John's lover. That's what hurt most, my own stupid myopia.

"I saw Don the other day," Jojo started before I could get a word in. "That man is finer than Italian wine!" She whistled then sipped her beer.

"Don?" How did she even know about him?

She smiled carnivorously at me. "The guy everyone said loved you to death?" She winked. "He looked very good. He would have made a better match for you, by the way."

I hated her, wanted to burn the smirk off her face with acid. But I would not let her see my anger. I shrugged.

"His bank balance was just not up to par," I said.

"Aah, yes. You love those trinkets John gives you."

"I wouldn't exactly call a Range a trinket," I said, smiling my own canine smile. Bitch!

But questions were starting to claw at me and draw blood. Did I really love John? Would he care if he found out that I had cheated on him? Was I a bad wife? Did normal couples stay this long without sex?

I realized how badly I want to stay married to him. "And he has fantastic taste in shoes," I said, trying to reassure myself.

Wicky had money, of course, but Jojo didn't seem to be getting any of it, and maybe that's why she wanted John.

"I know." Jojo smiled. There it was: her confession. I was just about to throw my whisky sour at her face, but then she added, "You don't know, do you?"

How dare she? I wanted to see the look on her face, so I blurted it out. "I know you are sleeping with my husband."

She laughed. She even clapped her hands while at it. I should have punched her, but the sarcasm in her laughter simply deflated me. Then she sobered up all over sudden and became very serious and leaned back into her seat. "You are such a child," she said, and it could have been Mama berating me for something. "Have you really never noticed how much time John spends with Wicky?"

"So what? They are best friends?" I said, feeling confused and tricked out of control of the conversation. "This is about you trying to steal my husband."

I was still seething, but Jojo had made me curious too. What did she know that I didn't? No matter how much time I spent with John and Wicky, together or separately, their friendship felt mysterious.

I saw pity in Jojo's eyes, and it made me panic. My heart was suddenly racing.

Jojo took my hand in hers. "I always thought you knew, Annie, and I figured if you didn't know, you would find out for yourself soon enough."

"Know... what?" She was frightening me now.

"You and I were chosen under different circumstances, but we serve the same purpose." She released my hand as if giving up on me. She sipped her beer and made me wait. "We are being paid to be beards."

I had never heard a crazier conspiracy theory. It was my turn to laugh.

"I know, I know..." she added, raising her hands. "I sound ridiculous because you've been having fire sex with Wicky for God knows how long."

My body went cold.

"You didn't think it was a secret, did you? Not that I care. It's what I like most about Wicky. The choice... the... freedom."

Everything seemed to blur. A machine at the bar went off and drilled into my head.

Jojo shook her head, deep trenches forming on her forehead. I could not stand to look at her, to see her pity, to deal with what she had just revealed. I looked all over the bar instead, desperately seeking eye contact with anyone else, but no salvation came.

Since meeting John and deciding he suited my plans, I'd been playing the role of a sweet, naïve and uncomplaining woman. I'd played the role so well; I had become that woman. Memories started connecting like pieces of a puzzle in my head. Wicky at our honeymoon hotel in Seychelles. Wicky always at our house. Wicky supervising the house John built for Mama. Wicky always hanging around at Muthaiga golf club, even when he'd told me several times that he hated golf. Wicky delivering the Red Range Rover with John, after John abandoned me on our anniversary. My birthday. That one time I found him in our bedroom stepping out of the shower, my husband's towel wrapped around his waist.

"Has John consummated?" Jojo asked, very much enjoying my discomfort.

"Please, it's been a year!" I fidgeted and took a long sip of my drink.

"Yes or no?"

A ball was growing in my throat and I tried to swallow it down. Thoughts of John and Wicky went around and around my head like a Tom and Jerry chase. Wicky had initiated the flirting. He had wanted to go shopping with me whenever John was away on business trips. He was always talking about how much he loved children, and how Jojo hated them. His kisses, his touch... Wicky's baby...

"He was John's best man at the wedding," I said, trying to stay afloat.

"Poetic, isn't it?" Jojo flashed me another of her blinding smiles.

"Why didn't you stop me?"

"Why would I want to do that?"

I started crying. Jojo asked for her bill.

"I should have chosen Don," I said as she picked up her handbag to leave.

"Oh, really?"

†

I sat alone at the bar, facing my empty glass for about an hour, before I drove to Wicky's home in Kileleshwa using the shortest route I could find on Google maps. The fools hadn't locked the gate. I parked behind John's silver Audi. My mind was clearer than it had been in the year I'd been married.

The door wasn't locked either. Their shoes stood side by side on the fluffy doormat. I wondered whether I really wanted to do this thing. Wasn't it easier to just ram the Range into the Audi several times? I removed my shoes at the door and neatly placed them next to my husband's. Then I walked into the house.

Wicky's was a well-furnished home, very masculine. Teddy Pendergrass was playing on the system. John's shirt was lying on the carpet, but his grey blazer lay neatly folded over the deep brown L-shaped couch. He had brought this same coat to Seychelles.

Our room had overlooked the sea. There had been rose petals on the bed. Champagne. And a sinful amount of Swiss chocolates. John had bought me the lingerie I'd worn that day. He'd watched me with satisfaction as I had tried on the tiny pieces, then he had asked me to wear my new red-bottom heels and wait for him. I had only realized where he had gone later on, when he had returned after many hours and passed out on our honeymoon bed, smelling of vodka.

In Wicky's house, I removed my blouse and gently placed it next to John's coat.

At the bottom of the stairs lay a pair of jeans. They looked like Wicky's. I slowly removed my short skirt and placed it next to the trouser. I could hear faint groaning from the upstairs.

My heart was pounding. I was now in my lace underwear.

I took the stairs, one at a time, remembering how Wicky came to visit me in the Church's waiting room on my wedding day. He'd said I was the most beautiful bride he had ever seen, before landing a light kiss on my lips. I had been shocked, but also pleasantly scandalized. I had felt desirable. His eyes had searched my soul, and his fingers caressed my exposed arm. I had wanted him.

Midway up the stairs, the wood creaked beneath my feet, but the groaning upstairs did not slow. At the very top was a pair of black Tom Ford underwear. John's. Could I seduce a man who looked at me as his sister? I unclasped my bra and dropped it next to the underwear.

The varying sounds of passion awakened an ache between my legs. I approached the room with the door slightly ajar. I watched them for a minute. They moved as one. My husband on his hands and knees on a blue quilted duvet cover. His best friend, our husband, standing tall, black and broad-backed. Lost in their own world. I, a spectator. An intruder, dripping wet. They had all I wanted.

I knew one of them might reject me, but I didn't know what I would do if both of them did. My courage faltered in the face of their unfettered passion, and I turned to leave, but I could not. I wanted them both. I looked down at my belly, still flat and yet, full of life. We were going to make a beautiful family.

I removed my panties and left them at the bedroom door, then I let myself into their secret.

Awuor Mugeni loves all kinds of art. Her main hustle is Graphic Design, and this is her first published story. She doesn't yet know why she writes, but she loves it. Connect with her on twitter as @yvadiva

The Harmonium

Sanaa Jabeen

"The harmonium makes no sound without effort, Sonia. It gives only what you put into its forty-two keys, and sometimes, if you're lucky, you can create life that is music. In, out, in, out, breathe Sonia, breathe like the harmonium and watch the magic unfold."

I was eight years old when my father gave me the 'harmonium is life' speech. We were in my childhood home in Farukh Nagar. It was twilight and guests were filtering in for my father's performance of sangeet, a musical tribute that he had performed weekly ever since he was a teenager. In the middle of greeting all his fans, he turned to me as if just noticing me, and seeing my awe at the crowd, gave me the speech. At that moment, I thought he was only mine and that he was the greatest father in the world. During the sangeet, I watched his knobbly hands fly over the keys of the harmonium and paced my breath to him.

Aman hated the music. He left to play soccer outside as soon as the guests began arriving and only returned when they were all gone.

When I was twelve years old, Aman held my hands and said that they looked exactly like our father's. This was why I was dad's favourite, he said.

"Sonu, it makes sense, na? If you look like him then, of course, he'll love you!" And with that, he shaved his head. His brown curly locks filled our bedroom floor, and to finish off the look, he took my baby powder and dusted his face. His eyes were a solid black, so different from my green. They looked hollow, lost in all the powder, and I felt I couldn't reach him. "Look Sonu, I'm Baba!" he yelled, stepping out of my reach.

I fell off the bed laughing. He took my shawl, wrapped it around himself like a sharwani and strutted around the room, barking orders and destroying everything in his wake. He pulled my books down from my shelves and with a new madness in his eyes removed all my clothes from the small cabinets and threw them around the room.

When Baba found us hours later, there was hair everywhere, and Aman was crying uncontrollably in the corner. He glanced at Aman, ordered the nanny to clean up and then turned to leave, pausing only to inform me that class would start in five minutes.

"I've put my soul in these keys, Sonu," he said as I played the harmonium clumsily. "You'll see."

I never knew whether Baba loved Aman or me, but sometimes, when we played the harmonium together, I felt that at least he liked me.

✝

I listened to the Delhi Orchestra for the first time when I was fourteen years old. We were visiting my mother's relatives, and to give us some 'much-needed character', Shenu Aunty decided to take us to watch the New Year Symphony.

Compared to the sleepy farm lifestyle of home, Delhi was a dream. The city reminded me of the beehives at which Aman and I used to throw stones: chaotic, harsh and ready to bite at any provocation. From the moment we stepped off the train, I knew this was where I wanted to be. I didn't know why, but it was going to be Delhi, and I was ready to join the chaos.

After dinner, over masala chai, Shenu Aunty mentioned the symphony. Everyone in the room said 'no', the uncles, the aunties, their children, all except me.

"I came to eat and party, not to sleep," one cousin said and was promptly slapped on the back of his head by his mother.

I looked to my dad, expecting his excitement to echo mine. I was wrong. He was angry in a way only Aman and I seemed to recognize. He grew real quiet, his eyes seemed smaller and his smile grew friendly, but to me, that smile meant a storm was on the way.

"Let the children have their fun, Shenu. Who cares about the so-called symphony?" he said.

"But Baba, you love music."

That was my first betrayal of him.

He turned to me slowly and clearly and loudly told me to never speak to him like that ever again. His voice cracked over us.

Still, Shenu Aunty took me to the symphony and made Aman join us, to give me company. Seated there in the dark of the gigantic hall, dressed in my best dress, I waited with a tight stomach. Aman was already bored and fidgeting in his seat, but I mirrored my aunt's attitude: quiet, attentive, excited. The curtains drew back and for a few moments, there was no sound, no movement. I felt a rush of delicious anticipation, the kind of waiting where nothing has yet ruined one's expectations.

A melody broke the silence. A violin, I recognized, with the support of a delicate flute, fluttered through the concert hall, teasing our ears before the main feature. That was the moment I understood what my father had been talking about all those years ago, the soul in the music. I was ruined, tears in my eyes and my hands gripping my brother's hand so hard he had to slap my hand away, but I didn't care. This was everything.

After the first song, I looked at my aunt, her eyes shining with tears and a wide smile on her face. She understood, my aunt, and in gratitude, I leaned my head on her shoulder. She ran her hand down my hair. I was happy in that moment, a moment interrupted by another melody, this one softer than the rest – a whisper in the shadows, slowly revealing itself. A violence of beauty and passion. A piano, I realized with a start, frantically searching for it. There it was. A woman sat at the back, so small I could barely see her, but there she was, playing with feeling and agony.

I knew then that this was my future I was looking at: my head bowed over the keys, my fingers making people weep with feeling that could not be named. It was my future, and it was sitting before me, unaware, unassuming.

That night after the symphony, Aman and I were sleeping on mattresses in the sitting room. It was late. I thought only about the music; my fingers moved with the sound I had promised myself never to forget.

"He'll never let you," Aman whispered to me abruptly.

"What do you mean?"

Aman looked at me and in the dark, I saw his profile and his eyes, less angry than usual, a rare softness on his face that most people never saw.

"Baba won't let you. I saw you at the symphony, Sonu. I might not get it, but I know you. You want this. You want to play the piano, not the harmonium. You want this life in the big city, with big dreams. You want people to see and hear you as Sonu. He won't let you, Sonu. Baba is… Baba is not going to let you."

I hadn't heard him talk like that in a while. The older Aman got, the quieter he became. I used to make fun that sometimes it was like he was invisible.

"You don't know that, Aman! Baba, he gets me. He loves music, like me. He'll be proud, you'll see. Remember what Baba says, Aman? These hands were made for music."

I held my hands up as if that was the only proof he needed.

Aman fell asleep, worried about me, I knew, but I was sure. Baba loved me, but more importantly, he loved music.

As quiet as Aman was, he was rarely wrong. Baba said 'no' and after a frightening fight at home, I stopped asking. Aman spoke to Shenu Aunty in secret and because of them, I was able to do piano classes at school and just like that, what might have been the worst three years of my life became the most important. I found myself in the keys. They just weren't the ones my father wanted me to play.

I could never ask Baba why he detested the symphony so much. Aman said it was because the musicians in it were better than him, and Baba could never let anyone, or anything be better than him. Shenu Aunty said it was because Baba was professionally rejected a lot when he was younger: "They rejected him so now he rejects them, Sonu."

On the last day of my finals, the principal called me into his office and instructed me to go home. I was eighteen years old. and the last day of school was what I had been waiting for. With Aman and Shenu Aunty's help, my piano classes at school and the harmonium classes at home had paved the way to Delhi. Everything was going to change, and I was ready.

I left school with a lightness I hadn't felt before. Shenu Aunty was waiting for me outside the school gate; I smiled wider.

"Shenu Aunty! I'm done!" I practically sang to her, hugging her tightly. She did not hug me back. Sensing her discomfort, I pulled back.

"What's wrong?" I asked her, worried. Had Baba found out about the piano classes?

She didn't reply. Her eyes were wide, and her lips trembled. She took my hand and led me to the car. We drove off in silence, and I looked out the window at the clouds; the monsoon season would arrive soon. All the way home, I thought about what I was going to tell Baba. I would tell him about the scholarship and maybe promise not to give up the harmonium. Maybe I could find harmonium classes in Delhi to make him happy, anything so that he would let me play the piano. With Shenu Aunty there, the chances of him screaming were slim, but when she left, his rage would likely ruin my plans to go DSA, the Delhi School of Arts, unless I handled him carefully.

Shenu Aunty drove while I panicked, but we didn't stop at the house. She parked a few gates away on the side of the road.

"Why did you park here?" I asked her, looking around. She was gripping the steering wheel, her breathing shallow.

"Something happened, Sonu... And I... I was asked to be the one to tell you because... I am the only one who should, apparently."

"You're scaring me, Ma. Is it Baba?"

"No, Sonu, it's not your Baba."

She turned to me, her eyes red.

"It's Aman."

A buzzing had started in my ear. She was talking but I couldn't hear her. The sound was too loud, and I covered my ears.

"Sonu! Sonu! Listen to me!" Shenu Aunty removed my hands from my ears. She was still speaking, but I swear all I could hear was screeching, although there were no other cars around.

"Sonu!" She shook me and I focused on her.

"Aman?"

She was crying.

"Yes, Aman. He... he, we just found out. He... He's gone Sonu. The workers found him in your dad's music room. Sonu..." She sounded like she was choking. "Sonu... He hung himself. He's gone Sonu, I'm so sorry, I'm..."

I didn't hear the rest.

☦

Years later, in another lifetime, someone was playing Jagjit Singh, in a coffee shop of all the places.

"Can you hear that?" I asked my friend Puna, one of my partners at the Delhi Orchestra. She looked at me over her coffee, her eyes unsurprisingly tired. It was one in the morning, and we had only just finished practice.

"What?"

"The ghazal? Can you hear it?"

"No yaar, I can only hear the sound of my career and love life going down the drain." She joked, but I wasn't in the mood.

"Puna, seriously! The Jagjit ghazal, the Kaagaz one? Can't you hear it?" I grabbed her wrist, forcing her to focus.

She closed her eyes, listening.

"Nope, I can't hear anything. Speaking of, I actually don't remember the last time I heard a ghazal," she said, "What about you?"

III

I could definitely hear it. A soft melody and a familiar voice accompanying it with the telltale sound of a well-played harmonium, a sound like no other, no matter where you looked. It was getting louder, how could she not hear it?

"Puna, listen to how loud that is!"

She looked at me like I was crazy.

"Sonu, I think you need sleep. We both do. Tomorrow morning, we can listen to as many ghazals as you want, okay?"

"No!" I replied sharply enough for her to lift her eyebrows, but I ignored her. It was so loud, I couldn't hear the buzzing conversations of the rest of the orchestra around us. Putting my hands over my ears, I left Puna and hurried outside, in need of fresh air.

It didn't help. My ears were hurting. I moved slowly to my car parked on the curb. Inside, I held myself and breathed the way my therapist had told me to, whenever I was having a panic attack.

In, out, in, out, breathe Sonia, breathe like the harmonium and watch the magic unfold.

"No, no, no, no, no, no," I told myself over and over again.

A sharp sound broke through my haze. My phone was ringing.

"Hello? Shenu Aunty?" I tried to keep my voice steady.

"Sonu Bacha, how are you?" Her voice was higher than usual. The ghazal was getting loud again.

"What's wrong?"

She was quiet. I bit my lip, my left hand automatically pulling at my hair.

"It's your Baba. He's sick. Sonu, I think he's dying. I was hoping you would…"

I tasted blood in my mouth. I walked through waking dreams.

"Sonu, it's your dad. I know Shenu talked to you. I want to speak to you. Call me."

"Sonia, have you spoken to him?"

"If you need a week off, Sonia, we can give you that. Just say the word."

"Sonia? Sonia? I was asking about your dad. Is he okay?"

"Sonu, it's been two weeks! I know you're getting these messages. I'm not… We're not asking you for anything. Just call him. Sonu, please."

✝

After Aman's funeral, an old teacher of his came to hug me and she said she was sorry for my sadness. I told her I wasn't sad. I was angry. It was the only thing I had said all day, but I felt tired after saying it. She was confused, her old wrinkled face tanned by the harsh sun of the day. After a beat, her confused face smoothed away and she said she understood, of course, we're all angry at the circumstances. No, I said. I'm not angry at the circumstances. I'm not angry at fucking god, hell, I wasn't even angry at my father, I was angry at Aman. I knew I was shouting; I knew I was being told to calm down, but she needed to know. I was angry at Aman. He chose to leave me, I screamed at the old woman, he CHOSE. I was angry, and I was always going to be angry.

Baba wasn't angry. He went straight to his music room and the harmonium played all night. All night, it rang in my ears, and I wanted to die. I wanted Aman to take me with him. I left that night and I refused to look back.

Aman chose to leave, so he did. I didn't know where that left me. If there was a god out there granting wishes, I prayed he would bring back Aman and take Baba instead.

†

I was in the hospital. Puna said she had found me in our shared bathroom, my shaved hair scattered all around me, my ears bleeding and my hands bruised and broken. I was screaming, she said.

"Screaming what?" I asked.

She was afraid, I could see.

"For it to stop. You said it was too loud."

I nodded.

"Sonu, you asked me to… You asked me to cut off your ears. You asked me to kill you." She was staring at my bandaged hands then at my hair.

I nodded again.

The doctors were keeping me under observation.

"Did anything happen?" they asked me. I told them my brother died.

That made sense to them, they said. Grief takes time.

I nodded. It took time.

"Your hands will heal but… we don't know if you'll be able to play again."

"Sonu… did you break your hands?" Puna asked me quietly after the doctors had left. "Did you want to break them, I mean?"

I nodded.

She was crying. "Why Sonu?"

I stared at the bandaged hands. I wasn't going to play again.

"Because they look like his. He only loves you if you look like him," I said, although I knew Puna would not understand.

†

Before I joined the orchestra, I went back home. I visited Aman at the cemetery and then went to see Baba. The harmonium played on while I stood outside the door. I told the workers to tell him I was there. They showed me to the kitchen, and I waited.

That was the last time I saw him. I wanted to laugh because Aman had played him so well: the white pale face, the bald head and the stoop from bending over a harmonium for too long. The lines on his face were set so deep, they reminded me of river bends. There was no joy in his face, nor in mine. I didn't know why I was there.

"Baba, I joined the Delhi Orchestra. I am going to be happy. That's all I wanted to tell you."

He was quiet, his hands ticking like he was playing an invisible harmonium.

I was about to leave when he spoke. His deep voice a rumble that I hated myself for missing. He was talking, and I wished he could sing to me, one last time. One last time, Baba, while it doesn't hurt, one last time.

"I never wanted this for you," he was saying.

"That's what you always said. Can't you move on?"

"Can you, Sonu?"

I stepped back. From his music room at the back of the house, I could hear his harmonium. An old ghazal of grief and loss, filling up the house. It was getting louder. Baba looked at me like he knew, like he could feel it too.

"Who is playing that?" I asked him.

He ignored me. "Remember ghazals, Sonu? What do you feel when you hear them?"

I shook my head, the ghazal mixing with the odd buzzing.

"Sonu, I asked what you feel?"

"I don't even know what that question means," I replied, my hands going to my hair. I needed to leave. Seeing him had been a mistake. "What do I feel? It's a song. It's a goddamn piano-"

"Harmonium."

"Who the fuck cares, Baba?" I couldn't hear myself, but I knew from the buzzing that I was yelling.

"Tell me, Baba, since you know everything, who the fuck cares about the 'breathing instrument of life'? Not me and definitely not Aman."

He flinched.

I laughed, even though there was nothing funny about this. His name hung in the air, the harmonium playing faster and louder, surrounding his name and breaking it into little pieces we could never get back.

"Really Baba?" I laughed on, "Afraid to hear his name? AMAN?"

He didn't reply. He was staring at me, scared, I realized. I stared back at him, my Baba, my teacher and my brother's murderer. It wasn't the first time I had thought it, and he knew it.

He turned to leave, then paused at the door.

"I wish you hadn't come home. I wish I didn't see you." He took a step to leave, but I didn't let him.

"I'm not saying sorry. I came here for a reason and now I'm done."

"You're done, Sonu? You said that five years ago and here you are, saying things you shouldn't, hearing things you're afraid to admit. You're not done." He was angry, his face red, foam around his mouth, his yellowing eyes more alive.

"You want my blessing? Tell me why! Tell me what you hear when you come into this house. Tell me, then you can be done. No, stop..." He held up his hand when I opened my mouth to speak. He was crying.

"Stop, Sonu. Stop talking. I am your father. That still means something."

And there it was. He was my Baba. I wanted to cry with him. Take his knobbly hands in mine and marvel, at how similar they were to mine. I wanted to hear him sing and play, I wanted to watch the magic. I wanted to die with Aman.

"It doesn't," I told him softly, the melody of the harmonium in the other room becoming ugly and painful to my ears. "He was my brother. That still means something, Baba."

†

Baba died the day they released me from the hospital. Shenu Aunty called me crying. He loved you, she told me. I asked her what they were going to do about the harmonium. She said Baba wanted it cremated with him. I said goodbye.

I went home. The music never stopped.

Sanaa Jabeen is a full-time reader who works as a strategist and a food magazine editor. "The Harmonium" is her first published work. Connect with her on Twitter and Instagram as @SanaaJabeen

The Night Runner

Gladwell Pamba

The blackness of night made him fidgety. His wife suggested that he go out to drink busaa with fellow men, to kill time. That way, he would stagger home at midnight and by the time he crossed the three bridges, if he managed at all, it would be minutes to one a.m. and he would be too tired to go disrupting the sleeping village with his runs. He heeded her advice, but by the third round of korokoro, he was still alert to his calling. His legs itched. He moved around the busaa den uneasily. An invisible hand tugged at him, one that only reached for him at night. Every noise around him boggled him, repulsed him, and he wandered into the dark leaving other drunkards absorbed in their banter.

By midnight, he knocked on the door of his hut. His wife sighed and reached for the simsim stored in a basket under their bed. She also brought out a broken piece of pot from under the bed and blew on the embers in the fireplace. She placed splinters on the embers and moved the three cooking stones wide apart, to place the broken piece of pot with simsim directly on the fire as the ritual dictated. She stirred the simsim with a wooden spoon. A few minutes to one a.m., her husband left the house soundlessly, smoke escaping through the open door. She remained in the dark stirring and seated on the low wooden stool. Her right hand became numb; she switched hands. Even as the fire went out, she continued stirring; the ash was hot enough. If she stopped or dozed off and burnt the simsim, he would get caught. She did this all the nights he was possessed.

He came back two hours later, entering the same way he had left. She did not light the tin lamp; she remained motionless after his entry. A few minutes later, she put the simsim aside and got into bed. He was still drenched and panting.

"Nobody met you?"

"No. Luck again."

"Not even a drunkard?"

"No. But tomorrow is the feast of Chiswa. I'm sure someone will stay out late at the anthill."

"What if they spear you? They have resolved to kill you if they catch you."

"Nobody wants this curse. No one is even ready to have a death on their head. All these people are timid rats. Anyway, profwesa said I have lumonya and if I don't stay warm, I'm going to die."

"Would you rather die?"

"Yes. For everything that it is worth, yes. I am tired, Kwamchetsi. Why don't you leak this to someone?"

"The curse won't go away, my husband."

"But what should I do now? Do you think I don't ever want to have a peaceful night like others? Do you think it is easy running in fields without any control of myself?"

He begged his wife to ensure she never got pregnant so that the curse would die with him.

†

Kukhu, still motionless in bed, screamed, "What do you want?"

Someone was running around our hut, stomping as if dancing to lipala. Mounds of mud fell off the hut's wall. The rest of us slept on the floor and huddled near my grandmother's sheep and calves. They were scared too; one of the calves let down dung. There was a loud bang on the door. We thought whoever was outside, our tormentor, had thrown a huge stone at it. We feared it would give in and leave us exposed like a conquered town. Mutendi was the first to scream and we followed suit.

"He will steal your voices if you keep screaming that way," Kukhu whispered hoarsely.

We cupped our hands over our mouths. The footsteps outside drew nearer to the wooden window directly above our sleeping position. My stomach was a hot piece of charcoal. I bit hard into my palm. The intruder outside farted loudly or produced a sound close to a fart. It was loud enough to scare Kukhu's chickens. They clucked as though a mongoose was lurking nearby. We cowered and hugged each other tightly, hoping to disappear into each other's bodies. The wild wind rustled the twigs and leaves in the trees outside as if a coven of witches were gathering to perform rituals in our homestead. The night runner was holding the world in his hand, and we were tiny creatures at his mercy.

Saulo whispered, "Is he going to kill us?"

Mutendi silenced him with a pinch. I wondered where Saulo got the balls to speak at such a stomach-churning moment. Injendi was breathing hot air on my neck. The night runner outside started clawing at the window and we screamed even louder. We imagined

121

his long dirty nails reaching for us through the wall. He then hit the window with a stick and some mud around it tumbled on us. The sheep kicked about, bleating. Saulo's scream rose above all of ours.

"Bayai omulosi iwe! Okhabhaa shina?" Kukhu shouted and started tapping her walking stick on the wall. "Don't you have mercy on an old dying widow, eh?"

The night runner threw what sounded like sand under the door. Then we realized it was not really sand he had thrown under the door but cockroaches. Kukhu wailed and cursed him, declaring that one day the sun would shine when he was still running around homesteads. We heard him laugh.

Kukhu only lit the tin lamp by her bed when she was sure the night runner had left.

Many people around Kimang'eti whispered they knew who the night runner was. I decided it could not be any of my friends' fathers, because they also complained about the night runner when we went to graze cattle and to swim in the river. Their fathers took them to the annual agricultural show, paid to have their faces painted and bought them colourful flutes and sunglasses. And to Chesoro Forest, and to see the Crying Stone with their own eyes. None of them would run around naked at night.

Excluding them removed ten men from my list of potential night runners. That left twenty men from our village. Of the twenty, three were pastors and seven were teachers. Chances of a teacher or pastor running around at night naked seemed close to nil. The ten remaining included two of my uncles. Fortunately, my lineage had never produced a night runner. The worst hereditary trait we had was being temperamental. The eight remaining men included our chief. He had been ordained by a spiritual leader who had thrown some cowries on the ground to see who the Ancestors had chosen to be our next Chief. There were also two people who had moved to Kimang'eti years ago, who were not really Kabrasi. One was a Maasai and the other one a Nandi, which exonerated them.

The last five appeared as unlikely: M'masi, an uncommitted coffin maker, thin like grass, was inebriated almost all seasons. It was not uncommon to find him sleeping in a ditch. What time would the alcohol leave his head for him to run around at night? During the day, when he did not have his bottle, he was a rained-on chicken. He went about hammering a nail here and tightening a bolt there in his yard. When night fell, he was a drunken moron, complaining that his business needed more customers.

Indangasi was a doctor at the dispensary and people referred to him as profwesa. He was the most learned fellow in Kimang'eti and as far as Kuvasali and Chimoroni. People consulted him even in matters that did not involve sickness and worshipped his opinions. They asked him about politics and what was happening around the world. His dispensary was always packed, not with patients, but with people listening to his wisdom.

Then there was Sunguti, whom Kukhu always suspected. He never closed his mouth. In funerals, he never spared the departed if they had some anti-social behaviour. He reminded everyone that the deceased was a prostitute, or a robber, or a selfish man. He seemed to know everyone's dark secrets. When my grandfather passed on, Sunguti said he died a poor man because he refused to marry a second wife and stuck to my lazy Kukhu. It was in everyone's mouth that Sunguti had tried match-making young women with my grandfather. But I thought that if Sunguti was a night runner, he would probably have told the world.

The last two on my list were crippled.

Some people were of the idea that the night runner was from the neighbouring Machemo or Chimoroni, because it had been decades since a lineage produced a night runner in Kimang'eti. But a night runner from Machemo or Chimoroni would have had to run a long way and risk the sun coming up before he got back home.

Whoever he was, I was sure he was one of us.

†

The next time the night runner returned, he plastered something on our door, something that sounded like mud. In a few seconds, the room reeked, leaving us coughing and spitting. Human excreta. Kukhu cried and called on our late grandfather to intervene. Why did he leave her to suffer in the hands of night runners? Was he happy now that she was suffering alone with her cursed grandchildren? I thought that maybe if my father were there, he would have chased away the night runner the way my friends' fathers did.

The next morning, we scrubbed down the door, vomiting at intervals. Where did he get such foul shit? Whoever it belonged to, his intestines were surely fermenting.

"I want my mother," Injendi said when Kukhu went to fetch more water from the borehole.

"You are stupid. Your mother does not want you," Mutendi said.

"Even you, your mother does not want you!" said Injendi.

"At least she comes to visit us. She will take us one day," said Saulo.

"I just want my father," I said.

"We don't have fathers! Did you not hear what Kukhu said?" Mutendi said.

"She cannot be our father. She is a woman," I said.

"But our fathers died, so she is our father," Mutendi said.

124

I could not talk with them any longer. I went and sat under the musemwa tree near Kukhu's hut, from where I could hear passers-by talking about the havoc the night runner had caused the previous night. One household had a worse night than most. Their window was not tightly shut and when he threw fresh shit at it, it flew open and the shit landed in a sufuria of vegetables.

The men decided to form vigilante groups to tackle the night runner. Young and older men were drawn from all households and assigned to watch out in turns. One group decided to have one man hide in a basket left outside. Once the night runner came, he was to pounce on him and blow the whistle. On that night, the first person's turn to hide in the basket came. He changed tactics and instead hid in the nearby bush as a last-minute decision of his own. Nothing happened for the better part of the night except mosquitoes drinking his blood and crickets screeching. At about one a.m., he saw movement from behind the house. The night runner tiptoed towards the basket and threw a huge stone inside it! He then took off at a devilish speed! In the morning, suspicion was high among the group members. How had the night runner known about the basket? The following night all men kept vigil and we slept well.

The night after that and many others that followed, the night runner stayed away. The rains came and seemed to have permanently disrupted his schedule. Planting season came and went peacefully. But when the crops were budding, someone began nipping off the young maize cobs. He trampled on the fields and scattered the maize on the ground. The aggrieved farmers swore to chop the culprit to pieces.

†

By this time, my friends had finished building their simbas because their fathers had helped them in fixing the thatch roofs, plastering and decorating walls with red and grey and white mud and finding them enough newspapers to beautify their new rooms. But even though Saulo and Mutendi helped me in mudding my simba, we took way longer than anyone else. I looked forward to having a hut of my own away from Kukhu's and being my own man. I promised Injendi that he would stay with me even though he wet the bed sometimes. I felt good but wished I had a father who would have bought busaa and slaughtered a fowl on the night I moved huts. Kukhu said it was not a must to do these things. But I imagined having a fowl slaughtered specifically for me, and me eating the special parts: the imondo and drumstick. Saulo would burn with envy and Mutendi would cry.

A week before it was complete, I lit a fire in the middle of my half-ready simba and added huge mupeli logs to burn till morning. Mupeli smoke chased away bad spirits. Several times that night, I made trips from Kukhu's hut to the simba to check the fire and back. It was a bright windless night. The light clouds took dreadful shapes. The moon skittered across the sky, occasionally getting swallowed by clouds then rising again. I was making my way out for the third time when I bumped into a stark-naked man just outside our door! He froze, and my legs grew weak momentarily. We then scattered in different directions, me screaming at the top of my voice, and he, running like a sprinter. I plunged into Kukhu's house and bolted the door. My cousins were practically dead with fear and did not stir. Only the sheep seemed to share in my predicament. They started bleating. Tiny insects danced in my blood. My heart was a loud isukuti drum. Only later did I realize the face I had seen was familiar, but I refused to recognize the man.

People in Kimang'eti said that if you saw a night runner's face, his curse would be transferred to you. The next night, I hugged my cousins tightly as we slept, afraid that I would get possessed and go night running. If it was discovered that I was a night runner, I would never marry a beautiful girl. I would marry a girl who had 'broken her legs' as a teenager, known men and childbirth. When I died, I would be buried at the corner of my own homestead, towards the gate. My armpits, my buttocks, my neck were all wet with fear that night. As time changed hands, my bowels boiled, and I felt I was going mad. Kukhu had not bought simsim to roast in case I became possessed and said it was better if I was caught on my first night out to save me from the misery of the curse. I felt she did not care for me and wanted me gone to reduce her burdens.

Unluckily for her, I slept well that night, and the curse did not transfer to me. Still, in the weeks that followed, I worried that it would come out later in my life, and I would one day suddenly throw off my clothes and run into the night.

✝

One morning, Mutendi, Saulo, Injendi and I were running to queue at the water point. Kukhu liked to wake us up as soon as the sun showed one tooth. Its rays were still soft, and the morning chillness was strong on our skins. As we trudged along the narrow road heading downstream, we heard Sunguti's husky laughter from his nearby homestead and many other voices. We decided the water could wait and ran to see why the noise. Sunguti was shouting at, rather than talking with, Marko and Imbiakha who kept nodding. Marko's eyes, like those of many others', followed the running man in Wera Tangata's maize field the way a praying mantis moves and bobs its head.

Laughter. Cheers. Excited voices. While some groups of men spoke in hushed tones and with lowered heads, Mwembula had a larger crowd around him, nodding in agreement to whatever he was saying. Someone asked him something and he responded passionately, his hands flying urgently, his head turning sharply from one listener to the other as if daring them to a fight. His listeners moved their hands and heads just as much.

The women stood behind the men. Some like Nasiche were ululating; a celebration was going down. Their laughter rose like smoke above the grass thatched houses. Their children, with eyes still swollen from sleep, tugged on their long loose dresses, asking for food. Some mothers sent their older children away to finish milking and tethering cows. The children threw a fit and the mothers beat them without reservation. Other mothers covered their babies' faces against the obscenity.

The man in Wera Tangata's maize field was naked. He kept alternating between walking and running. He made countless laps. Sweat glistened all over his body in the morning sun. His chest was tiny and hairless like a teenager's. His thighs were ashen, thin sticks. Clothes truly save people's anatomical shortcomings. He was more bone than flesh. No wonder he had such speed and agility at night. The one man who had attempted to run after him one of those nights had described his speed as demonic.

It was M'masi. He was bewitched and in a trance, moving around the maize farm and not looking us in the eye. I could not look him in the eye, anyway. His eyes were wide open. His dark, shrivelled penis dangled like an amulet. Scattered on the ground were budding maize cobs smeared with human excreta. At first, people wrinkled their noses and spat because of the foul smell. However, minutes later, they were comfortably drowning in excitement.

"Someone find Wera Tangata please!" said one village elder, not addressing anyone in particular. No one budged.

The bodaboda riders laid their bicycles and motorcycles horizontally by the roadside and joined in the buzz. Some were honking, firing up the atmosphere. People composed a song describing the naked man's laughable anatomy. Mutendi, Injendi and Saulo and I joined in the song, clapping and dancing:

Ndumbu ndumbu yee M'masi!
Se ya khomera ta!
Khafuana khakokho!
Wui! Wui! Amba maayi, amba papa!
Amba nakhufiala, amba bhoosi
Itse mulole omulosi M'masi!

Laughter filled the air and we repeated the song that called everyone to come and witness the shame. That M'masi was a chicken without feathers, a body not fit to be a true man's. Was that a penis or a pinkie?

More than anyone there, I was happy M'masi had been caught. I thought there was now no chance of the curse transferring to me. I didn't hate M'masi — he was just the village drunk. But I knew if Wera Tangata did not come to release him from the trance, he would die from walking and running for many hours. And the curse would die with him.

An hour later, word had reached Chimoroni and Machemo, and people from there arrived in armies like grasshoppers. It had been ages since all the villages assembled. Even funerals never brought so many people together.

They pushed past us to see M'masi's rigid buttocks stuck on his bones in a shapeless way, giant knobs knees and his tuft of pubic hair, a brown overgrown knot. The ugly hair grew up to his belly and down to his thighs. He was a caveman in his nakedness.

Everyone was talking at the same time:

"It serves him right!" Ngome said and added that M'masi was lazy.

"Someone having the audacity to smear faeces on doors and crops is not lazy. In fact, he is very hard working!" said Mwembula.

"Now his coffin business has one more customer."

"But who will marry his widow after this?"

"If I was born with that curse, I would kill myself, than let people kill me."

The elder shouted, "Where is Wera Tangata?"

"He went to Sigalagala," his son said. "He is not coming back this week, obasia."

It was Wera Tangata's home where M'masi had thrown shit that landed straight in a sufuria of vegetables. Wera Tangata had taken the shit to a witchdoctor and acquired strong witchcraft to trap the night runner.

M'masi's wife pushed through the crowd, shoving, cursing, shouting,

"Have you people no shame? Do you think it is his fault?"

Momentarily, people hushed, cleared a path for her, but when she reached the front row, strong hands gripped her as she tried to cover M'masi's nakedness. Was it not her fault that she had burnt the simsim and he had been caught? Was it not his own fault that he had not kill himself and died with the curse, on his own terms?

She wailed, threw herself on the ground, and screamed M'masi's name, but he did not look her way.

I noticed that Kukhu was watching us in silence, supporting herself on her walking stick. She was not amused. Instead, her face looked sad and worn out, like old sisal sack.

That was when I realized people were throwing quizzical looks at me. Their whispers made my skin crawl.

Then I saw it. M'masi had a huge birthmark on his thigh, just like the one I had.

Gladwell Pamba is a high school teacher of English and Literature and blogs at chingano.com. In 2019, She won the Afreada x Africa Writes short story competition and was longlisted for the

Writivism Short Story Prize. Connect with her on Facebook as Gladwell Pamba and on twitter as @GladwellPamba

The Syce

Shalom Ndiku

My Lord,
I am writing this letter to you because the lawyer representing us is saying to me if I write to you, you may forgive me for the wrong I am doing. I am not wanting forgiveness.

I am wanting to write and tell you the truth. My truth.

I will break the promise I made to my brothers and sisters not to tell, but for me, it is important you understand.

Bad is the opposite of good. Even me I am knowing that. But me, Thuku, I am not bad person. Bad person does something bad when having no reason. Me I had reason. I had very good reason, even Kinyanjui will be saying my reason is good when I tell him. Kinyanjui is my one brother, I am bigger in age, but he is bigger in body. My mother is saying he was always hungry when he is baby, making her breasts dry and empty like sorghum sacks in the time when it is not raining.

When I am small, like Kinyanjui's boy now, who is having a name like my father, Kiragu, my father was liking to ask me to help him do the work in the big farm near our small farm outside Fort Hall. Kiragu was the boss of many horses belonging to Mr. Rudwell, the mzungu, like you My Lord. Mr. Rudwell is mostly a good mzungu, but sometimes I am seeing him forcing my father when Kiragu is tired. Maybe the mzungu is just liking his workers to not stop working no matter what. Every day when I finish the school, I run, with the sun following behind me, very fast to Mr. Rudwell's stables to help Kiragu. After many sunrises, and days of going to church, and moons, and even after many rain and dry times, I am becoming horse expert. Even Mr. Rudwell is knowing this about Thuku. This time Kinyanjui is working in the kitchen with my mother. That is why his skin is soft like the inside of ripe yellow mangoes and his fingers gentle like those cold meat sticks Mrs. Rudwell is giving us to cook for breakfast every birthday of Jesus.

When Kiragu is going to sleep in the ground, Mr. Rudwell is saying that I become the syce like Kiragu. My mother is saying that my father is going to sleep because he was sick and Mr. Rudwell was refusing to make him to stop working with the horses even when he is coughing and blood is coming from his mouth. She is saying this, her face is folding like when you are trying to give a dog grass to be eating and it is saying no. She is mixing hot water and flour for millet in the kitchen with smoke everywhere, and it is smelling like millet is burning, but I know the burning is in my mother's heart because she is thinking about Kiragu. I am remembering one day coming from school and hearing Kiragu asking Mr. Rudwell to go see a doctor, but because the doctor is far away and it will take almost seven sunrises to go and come, Mr. Rudwell is saying no.

My mother is telling me a story when she is mixing the flour and water. She is saying the father of Mr. Rudwell's father came to take this land from Kiragu's family and he did not give us even one cowrie shell, one chicken or even that round silver the mzungus are liking. My mother is almost to crying when she is saying this I am feeling like when the sun is gone and there is no moon inside the night.

I want to cry also for Kiragu, my heart is almost exploding like those lights in the sky Mr. Rudwell and Derrick, the boy of Mr. Rudwell, burn every time a few sunrises after the birthday of Jesus. The ones which are making the horses to almost to become sick in the head because animals they are not liking exploding skies. But I am now head of the house, so no crying.

She is saying again, "We are living here on small farm and mzungu on big farm. But big farm was ours. That is what Kiragu is telling me."

My Lord, I am not saying all mzungu men are thieves, but many of your people are taking our land and not asking us.

After what my mother is saying, now I am knowing why my father was liking me to help him — so I can help Mr. Rudwell when Kiragu is sleeping. I now become the boss of the horses. All of them. Zev, the black boy one with metal under his shoes that is always making noise when he is walking on dry ground. Storm Dog, the brown boy one who when the sun is shining on his coat, I am covering my eyes with my hand like I am looking at fire. Burma, the white girl one that only Mrs. Rudwell is climbing and likes to eat mostly carrots. Aristidos, the boy one which is the colour of the soil when it rains big, who I am talking to using the voice in my head and it is like he is understanding. Genuine Racer, the small boy one for Derrick, which does not like to be taking a bath and we fight every week, but I am always winning because Kiragu is teaching me how to make a horse not be a fighter. I am wishing that we can talk using the voice in my head like I am doing with Aristidos, but I am thinking Genuine Racer in his head has only slow wind and stones.

My Lord, are you having horses? If you are having, you know they are the most good animals that the ancestors are teaching us to live with.

It is because of horses that I do the bad thing for good reason.

One morning Kinyanjui is sick a lot and vomiting also a lot like he has eaten all the rotten mangoes on the ground in Mr. Rudwell's farm. I take him to the doctor near the Sattima mountains in Nyandarua. In the morning, Mr. Rudwell is refusing that I go because the horses are only listening to me in that whole farm. But when he see my mother is crying and calling the name of Kiragu and falling on the ground, Mr. Rudwell is feeling bad and he agrees we go. He say he will be using Muli, the syce for the neighbour Lady McEwan, to help him with the horses.

We go with our legs — it is far like how it is if God said we must all walk to heaven. We sleep two times on the road before we are arriving, tired like the horses when they have to carry Mr. Rudwell's brother Seth because he is big like a pig that has swallowed all the other pigs in the East African Territory. I hope you are laughing My Lord, I am a good joker. Between the sun coming up and going down, Kinyanjui is vomiting more than five times. But soon, we are reaching at the doctor.

We enter the office to see her. Yes, her. The doctor is a woman. She touches Kinyanjui with hands looking like a very boiled potato. She is also saying he should put his finished food in a small mkebe, so she is seeing what is making the vomit. I don't know why she is asking for finished food from behind, yet vomiting is from in front, from mouth, she should ask for Kinyanjui's saliva, but I am not doctor so I keep my thinking where it belongs: in my head. The sun is now in our faces when we sit waiting for the Mrs. Doctor outside with other sick people like Kinyanjui.

When we are still sitting, I hear noise of metal hitting the ground four times quickly, repeating fast. Rrrap. Rrrap. Rrrap. Rrrap. I am listening carefully. It is a horse. I am knowing even before I see. Then I am seeing it. It is coming fast to us, like it is running away from a man with a big panga that is a butcher for horse meat. There are many people waiting like me and my brother for Mrs. Doctor. Men like me Thuku. Women like mother. Even small children like the little Kiragu. The running horse will run at all of us and it will be bad.

I stand up before I am thinking, then like big Kiragu is teaching me, I make the noise like a kanyua njui — the bird wearing a green hat, red shirt, black coat and white trousers. Kiragu was teaching me the secret to make a horse that is very mad to not be mad anymore. I cry loud, but at same time soft, I am putting my two hands up with one leg far from another. I must look big, I try very much, but I can only be big like Thuku. I wish I can be big like Mr. Rudwell's brother, Seth, or even like Kinyanjui. I am hearing Mrs. Doctor coming out because the sick people outside are making noise, they are seeing Satan in the eyes of horse when it is running to us. Kinyanjui is looking like vomiting again.

I do not stop crying like the kanyua njui. The horse is now seeing my eyes and I am seeing her eyes. She is looking like there is death inside her, she is also looking like Burma, the horse for Mrs. Rudwell. She is not running fast now and is starting to stop, the Rrrap Rrrap is now not fast.

"You'll get knocked to the ground," Mrs. Doctor is screaming to me.

I look back to her face and it is looking like a plum that is half a moon away from becoming ripe. She is wanting to come, but I shake my head so that she sees each of my ears two times. But I know horse better than she is knowing me. Slowly, the horse looking like Burma is not running. It is walking now. It is stopping so close I can taste in my nose that it was eating sticks of maize before Satan entered inside it. My hands hold the face and I go to the ear on the side of the face facing the sun, then I am singing:

Kanyoni kanja, kanyoni kanja
Gekugwa nja na mitheko
Ndakoria atiri, ndakoria atiri
Wamichore watinda ku?
Ndatinda Koiri, ndatinda Koiri

I am the good man that day, My Lord. Mrs. Doctor is happy. Everyone who is sick is happy also. She gives Kinyanjui medicine and she is telling him to return home with the eggs and bag of sorghum my mother was giving us to tell her thank you. Kinyanjui is going home alone because me I am now remaining. Mrs. Doctor is saying I will be the syce in her farm. I say yes because Mr. Rudwell is not giving me any shillings, just food for me, Kinyanjui and mother. But Mrs. Doctor is saying she gives me not just food, but also 3 shillings every moon. She is also writing a letter to Mr. Rudwell asking for his yes or no for me to be the boss of her horses. Later, when I am already working for four sunrises, a letter is coming back with a sick woman from near Fort Hall saying yes, he is sad I am not his horse boss like before, but he gives Mrs. Doctor a yes.

†

My Lord, I am the boss of the horses at Mrs. Doctor for many dry and rainy times. She is the wife of Mr. Ruck and they are having a small boy Michael. He is small, not having a lot of meat on his bones, and always smiling, like Kiragu, but his skin is white and becomes like a roasted pig when it is very hot. Kiragu's skin is always black when it is hot. Mrs. Doctor and Mr. Ruck are having many horses that I have to use two of my hands two times to count them. There is Tiny Dancer, Flying Swallow, Half Rainbow, Strutting Behind, Black Bee, Lander, Sheer, Overcomer, First Aider, Borrowed Time, Checker, Palmer, Flamingo, Wild One, Special Wings, Rook, Royal and Continental. The horses for Mrs. Doctor are tall, big, black, white, having a lot of meat, some not having a lot of meat, fast, even faster, and they are liking to eat different things. Some are liking grass, some are liking bananas, others are liking the sticks of the sukuma wiki, others are liking the covers of the beans. The one which is running when Kinyanjui is coming to see Mrs. Doctor is Borrowed Time because she is sick in the head since she was girl horse and the horse doctor is saying she will sleep soon, but she is not sleeping. Because I am singing Kanyuni Kanja for her when I am first coming here, she is now my best horse.

My Lord one night I am in the house for the workers where I am sleeping with the men like Paulo the cook, Musa who helps Wanja the lady for cleaning, who also is cleaning with Nyokabi and Mumbua during the day. I am also sleeping there with people like me who are working in the shamba and with the other animals that are not horses, like Karanja, Naaman, Nehemiah and Petero, who I am the boss of because he helps me with the horses. Ruth is also working in the shamba, but she is sleeping in another house for women, where also Wanja, Nyokabi and Mumbua are sleeping.

I am hearing a noise on the door of where the men are sleeping and when Petero is going to open, it is Nyokabi.

I am tired and if it was not Nyokabi but another person, I was going to sleep. The reason I am tired today is because in the morning Petero and me we took Michael to ride his horse, Black Bee, and I was on Palmer. But when we are there, Michael is falling badly, and I am thinking he has broken the bone in his hand. I carry him for many steps, I am running and running until I feel like I am running in water and carrying big stones and not this mzungu boy. When we are getting to the house, Mrs. Doctor is leaving her sick people and running to us to take him and Musa is helping her. No one is asking about me, my legs are like they have been put in the fire for cooking and there is no water to remove the fire. But when I am seeing Nyokabi now in the men's house, my energy is coming back.

My Lord, do you have a wife?

I am not looking for a wife when I come to Mrs. Doctor's, but I am very happy when Nyokabi is looking at me every morning smiling, every afternoon smiling and every night smiling since I have come to work here. Even once we are eating and she comes to sit with me, so close I am feeling her leg pushing my leg and she is not moving it because I think she also is liking it. She is telling me about how the mzungu men killed her father because he is refusing to give them his shamba. I am telling her about Mr. Rudwell and how he is forcing Kiragu to work even when my father is sick. When she is hearing this, Nyokabi is angry for me and I am feeling like inside me it is boiling. Another time she comes to me and puts her hands on my shoulder when no one is looking, saying she wishes we can do something about the mzungu people and I tell her I am agreeing, because my mother is saying this land was always for us, not for the mzungu. The whole time Nyokabi is telling me this, she is putting her head on my other shoulder. I am remembering this for two days of going to church. I am not washing that shirt because it is smelling like the milkfat she is putting in her big hair, until Paulo is complaining that my shoulder is smelling like sour milk that is becoming bad. Tonight, she is smiling very big, her teeth are showing like the many windows of a house full of milk in it. I am thinking I will ask her if she is wanting to marry me.

"Thuku, come. I am wanting to talk to you." Her voice is sounding like birds singing after the rain is finished.

I stand up and go to the door, which is bringing in cold air, but I am feeling hot inside. I am seeing Naaman and Musa smiling at me and Musa is even closing and opening one eye quickly. But Paulo, his smile is upside down like he is not happy for me. His mother is not ever teaching him to smile. It is good Paulo is not smiling because his teeth are looking like he is eating mud mixed with squeezed caterpillars and he will never find a wife like I am going to find now with Nyokabi. I am following her outside, my almost wife.

"Follow me," she is saying. "I am wanting to ask you something important."

Important is marriage, I am knowing that, My Lord.

She is walking like she is not afraid of the night. We are walking for many steps, until we are near the stable for horses, I am hearing Half Rainbow and Rook making noises because they are not liking sleeping. Nyokabi is stopping and looking at me. The moon is big and I am seeing her eyes, which are like those of a baby horse when it is born and are making me feel I am looking at how our big mother Mumbi was looking like when she was young, even before she was marrying our big father Gikuyu.

"Nyokabi, thank you for coming. I was going to ask you first, but you are not afraid to be telling me you are wanting me to be your husband," I am saying.

She starts laughing, not with a big noise, but if it was not night and we were not hiding from others, Nyokabi would be laughing loud like she was looking at two heads coming out of my neck. I am feeling like I am not knowing what is happening, but I am not having time to think because out of nowhere in the night I am seeing many men coming to me. They are not the men workers; I am not knowing them.

"Nyokabi, what…" but I am not having anything to say.

"Thuku, see our brothers."

The men are now close. The boss of the men is a short one. I am sure if it was day, I was going to see white hairs spreading around his head like that of maize because is he is very old.

"Are you Thuku?" he is asking.

"Yes, I am Thuku son of the sleeping Kiragu, son of Muigai. I am from Murang'a."

I am looking at him, but I am also looking at Nyokabi. Those eyes I was seeing the niceness of a baby horse are now not inside her. Instead I am seeing the badness of a big black snake, telling me the opposite of truth to make me think she is wanting to be a wife. I am wanting to hit her like I hit Continental when he puts his head through the fence and eats Mrs. Doctor's vegetables when those are only for the mzungu.

The short man is pointing to some of the men with him and they run into the darkness, he is telling them to look around, so no one is coming.

"Open the horse house," Nyokabi is saying. "You said that when I want to do something about the mzungu I should tell you."

I open. Before we are going in, I am seeing Naaman and Musa coming. They are carrying leaves of a banana tree and a small animal, I am not seeing what it is, but it is not breathing. I am not knowing what is happening, why are Naaman and Musa outside?

"Naaman, what is happening?" I am asking him when he is nearing, and I am smelling the goat he is holding.

He is saying, "It is time."

"Time for what?"

"To see if you are a real man," the short man is saying. "Let us enter the horse house."

"Stable," I am telling him in English.

He looks at me, nothing on his face, showing he is not understanding English words. My Lord some of my people are being stupid when it is coming to English words.

I enter. Nyokabi, Namaan and Musa are entering behind me then the remaining men the short man is having also are entering the stable. One of them is closing the door slowly. It is now more dark, but Nyokabi has made a small fire inside that is not scaring the animals. I am surprised because it is appearing this woman is a spirit and I was not knowing. I am seeing the orange light on the faces of Continental and Tiny Dancer because they stay near the door. We sit on the dry grasses of the horses, in a round shape. Musa is putting the banana leaves in the middle and Naaman is putting the goat on top of the leaves. The short man is removing a knife and cutting small meats of the goat and he is giving everyone. I am the last he is giving to and when I hold it, I am feeling the warm blood in my hands. I am knowing the animal has been killed in this night.

"We must fight for this land that is ours."

He is talking now like God has entered inside his body and the short man has no strength to do anything but let God be the talker. Now all the horses are not sleeping anymore, I am even seeing Rainbow listening like she is understanding our language Kikuyu, moving her head up and down.

He is continuing, "The mzungu took the land without caring that the Kikuyu were there. They do what they want with the land. Our land."

The short man is now standing, but because he is short our necks do not have to look up very far. He is walking behind all of us, the blood from the goat meat is falling on my neck. It is now cold like the short man's hands have been in the rivers that bring down the water from the white stone on Mount Kirinyaga.

"The mzungu came here and is just saying the land that we can see until the end of our eyes is his?" he is asking. "Without even asking for us to say yes or no. Without even giving us one shilling?"

He is walking behind us still, but when he comes to me again, I am moving a little so cold blood is not falling on my head again and he is going behind me without any blood falling on me. The blood is falling on Naaman, but he is not moving, like he does not feel it, but I know he is feeling it.

"Some days ago," the short man is saying, "a Kikuyu man is taking cows in the big land of a mzungu because the grass there is long and green. But when the thief of our land, that mzungu, is seeing the Kikuyu and his cows, he starts to beat him like a small boy until he is sleeping," he continues. "Last moon, another man is taking his cows and is shot in the head in the Kiambu hills. He is also sleeping. But that land is for his people."

I am feeling sick. I am remembering that Mr. Rudwell and even Mrs. Doctor are doing bad things to our people. I am always been working for the mzungu, they are making me believe they are good people, but when the sun is going down and the moon is rising, they are thieves of our land. Nyokabi is looking at me, and I am almost forgetting that I am not happy with her because her face is beautiful.

The short man stops walking, he is looking at Tiny Dancer, thinking. He is waiting for some time then he is saying, "Our people are suffering. We are suffering because our land is taken by the mzungu and we are slaves on our land. Will we sit and just wait?"

No one is saying yes or no. Everyone is looking at me.

"Thuku," the short man is asking, "what will you do? Your father, Kiragu wa Muigai, was made to work by the mzungu but he was sick and eventually went to sleep."

I nod, but I look at Nyokabi and I can tell she is the one who is telling the short man about Kiragu and Mr. Rudwell.

"Will you fight?"

I know I am a Kikuyu, our land was ours always, because God gave it to us for free. But the mzungu is coming and he is saying it is now his, like the mzungu is now God.

"I do not know how to fight," I am saying, quietly. I am having fear hiding in my chest.

"Fighting is easy, we will teach you. But before you fight, you must join us."

The short man is stopping his walking and is sitting in the space he was before he started walking. My hand is tiring of holding the goat meat, it is starting to smell bad like when it is dry for long and there is no water for the animals, and they sleep until they are bones. Oh, My Lord, the smell I am not even wishing on my worst enemy. It is making the hairs in your nose run away into your throat.

"Stand up, Thuku," the short man is saying strongly.

I stand. I hear kicking from one of the horses, maybe Strutting Behind, because she likes kicking when she is fearing.

"Say after me," he is saying.

"I will not tell secrets of our Society," he is saying.

I am repeating.

"I will not help the Government of the mzungu to catch members of our Society."

I am repeating.

"I will not sell our land to strangers."

I am repeating.

"Good," he is saying. "Now we go to the second part. All of you stand up."

They are standing up, like me. The short man is holding the meat up in the air and is closing his eyes, then he is saying things I do not understand very fast like he is in pain, as if there are red ants climbing up and down his body and someone is pouring honey on him. The others start doing the same, so it is just me with my hand down. They finish and the short man is eating the meat, which is not cooked and Nyokabi, Naaman and Musa, and also the other men, all eat the meat. They are looking at me, waiting for me to eat. I am looking at the meat. I am noticing it was red when it was cut, but now it is looking like there is little ash inside the meat.

I am closing my eyes and stopping the air from entering my nose, then I put all of it in my mouth. The meat is soft and is tasting like meat is usually tasting but with blood, maybe I can even eat more. The short man is walking to me and putting his hands on my shoulders, leaving some blood on my white shirt on top of where my left shoulder is, but it is okay because even if the smell of Nyokabi was there, I would not want it again.

"Now, Thuku, I want you to repeat again."

I am nodding. He is looking like a different man now, as if the sickness in the head of Borrowed Time is now inside his head.

"If I am asked to by the Society I will kill a mzungu," he is saying, in a voice that is strong like when you shout inside a big empty gourd.

The goat blood in my mouth is now feeling like it is starting to boil on my tongue and down where it goes to my stomach.

"Thuku?"

I look at the short man, his mouth is smelling like a latrine that is full and you need to dig a new one.

"If I am asked by the Society, I will kill a mzungu," I am repeating.

When I say this, I do not feel bad, I feel like I should do this, not for me, but also for Kiragu, and mother, and Kinyanjui. I even feel like I should do it for Nyokabi's sleeping father.

"If I am asked to, I will kill a Kikuyu who is against our Society, even if it be my mother or my father or brother or sister or wife or child," the short man is saying.

Louder now and with no fear, I am repeating. The short man and even Nyokabi with her small lips, are smiling at me. I am smiling back at her, maybe she was wanting to marry a member of the Society. My Lord, maybe there is hope for Thuku, I am thinking.

"If I am asked to, I will hide the body of a murdered person, so no one is finding it."

I am repeating.

"Welcome to the Society, Thuku. Naaman, Musa and Nyokabi will tell you what you need to do. We now have four of you in this farm and are ready for work."

†

After five moons, Petero is also joining the Society, My Lord. The short man is coming back at night to Mrs. Doctor's farm to visit two times. The last time he is giving us arrows, spears and knives from the Society's bosses up in Sattima Mountain. Naaman is hiding the knives and arrows where the goats are staying, and I am putting the spears in the grass that the horses will not eat until the next dry season which is many moons away. We are meeting every day inside the stable, sitting inside Tiny Dancer's room because she went to sleep last moon when bringing her baby horse. We have said yes that we will do the thing the bosses want us to do, it is dangerous, but we will do it.

The day we do it, we have said we will wait until it is nighttime so that no one has any work, maybe just Musa because Mrs. Doctor may say he is washing the dishes. I go back to the sleeping area. Paulo and Nehemiah are talking loudly at each other. Naaman and

147

Petero are listening but not talking. I do not want to do arguing with Paulo or Nehemiah.

I see Naaman and I tell him, but only with my eyes, that I am ready. He stands up and comes. Petero follows him.

"Where are you going, you will not eat? Wanja is making roasted sweet potatoes," Paulo is asking.

"We are coming, there is grass I want to carry from the back of the stable to the front but tomorrow I think it is going to rain, so I want Naaman and Petero to help," I am telling Paulo.

Paulo and Nehemiah continue talking loud at each other. Naaman, Petero and me leave their noise. We do not worry about them.

When we are outside, Naaman goes to the goat house and me to the horses. Nyokabi is waiting with Petero when we are returning with the knives and arrows and spears. We are walking and the four of us look to the window in the big house where Musa is washing. He is holding a big round white plate up then is putting it down.

The signal. Now is the time.

Naaman is looking at me and is saying, "Thuku."

I am running to the house, slowly first, but fast like Lander is the one carrying me on her back because she is the fastest horse. Mr. Ruck must be believing me. At the door, I hit on it very hard, like I am wanting to break it into small woods to start a fire with.

"Open Mr. Ruck! Open! Mrs. Doctor, there is Mau Mau outside! Naaman has caught him!"

I am looking behind and I cannot see Naaman, Petero and Nyokabi. I am hearing the legs of someone coming from inside, they are coming to the door and it is Mr. Ruck wearing his suit for sleeping at night that looks like the sky, it is even having clouds. He is holding a gun. I am feeling scared inside like maybe he will shoot me with it, but the short man was telling us that we should not look like we are scared, otherwise the mzungu will be knowing.

"Where the bloody hell are they?" he is asking and pointing the gun to the night.

I am pointing and he opens the door, going to the night. I am walking behind him, pointing still.

"There."

He is walking for a few steps; I am feeling my heart beating inside loudly like when Ruth is beating the drums at church when we are all singing Cha kutumaini sina.

When I know he is not knowing, my hands go to his neck and I am pressing hard, like when I am climbing a tree with no branches and I am not wanting to fall.

Naaman comes with a panga and he hits Mr. Ruck in the legs. Again, he hits him.

Petero is taking the gun, but he is not knowing what to do with it.

"Stop it! What are you doing, Thuku! Naaman!" shouts Mrs. Doctor.

Musa is coming from inside the house and he also holds Mrs. Doctor from the back. We do not go to her. She is fighting, but Musa is big, I am confused why he is a worker for the house and not for the animals or the shamba. His name is even Njogu.

Naaman is having a big firewood and he is putting Mr. Ruck on it.

Petero is using a spear and puts it inside the chest of the mzungu.

Naaman is using the panga again, is hitting Mr. Ruck.

The noise coming from Mrs. Doctor's mouth is like when you take a sheep and cut it, but the knife is not a good knife, so it is suffering. I like Mrs. Doctor, but I know she and Mr. Ruck are taking our land and they must return it.

Wanja comes screaming from the night. I cannot hear what she is saying because even her she is not knowing what it is. I close my eyes because I do not want to see what Naaman is doing, but even when I close my eyes, I am hearing the sound.

Thwack! Thwack! Krack! A bone, then again I am hearing a big Krrrrack!

Nyokabi is holding Wanja back and we are seeing Paulo and Nehemiah running to us shouting.

"Stop!"

"What are you fools doing?"

Naaman stops and it is quiet, but we can hear Mrs. Doctor now crying like a puppy when you are kicking it.

Naaman is saying to Paulo, "It is the responsibility of our people, stopping these thieves from stealing the land of our fathers and grandchildren."

"Stop it," Paulo is shouting.

I am not hearing Mrs. Doctor crying anymore and when I look, I see Musa is making her head to look back behind her, which a head of a human cannot do like it is an ostrich. She is sleeping now.

I turn and see Paulo is running to Musa like he is mad. I pick up the spear that Petero was using and I put it up so when Paulo is running, he is running into the spear. Paulo is running so fast that the spear is entering his chest like a hot knife when you are putting it in the sheep fat.

The women are screaming.

Petero and Naaman are hitting Paulo with pangas.

The women are running away. They are seeing that we are not afraid of making Kikuyu to sleep if they are wanting to be friends with the mzungus like Mrs. Doctor and Mr. Ruck.

We are now in the house looking for shillings and other things that are good and the bosses will be happy if we are returning with them. Musa looks to me and his eyes go up, telling me to go to the room up in the house. I look at Naaman, he is also looking up with his head, telling me also to go with his eyes. I am afraid to go upstairs, but I must.

"Hurry up. Nehemiah and the women will go to the police post. Finish quickly," Naaman is saying. He then using his head asks me to go up and finish the boy, Michael.

†

My Lord, the drops you are seeing in this page of my letter are from my eyes removing tears. I cannot finish the rest, but you are knowing it already. It is the truth which I should tell you because you and your people should know it.

Our land, you mzungu people stole it. You stole it. Mr. Rudwell he stole it from Muigai's father, now we are on the small farm, with nothing, but Mr. Rudwell has everything. Why? I am asking.

My people will fight for the truth until you are leaving us and giving the freedom you must return back to our people.

That is the truth.

Thuku Maina Kiragu
19th December 1955

Shalom Ndiku is a lawyer by profession and writer by passion. He has co-created, written and produced two television shows and is currently researching stories from Kenya's forgotten colonial era to generate material for historical fiction he believes the new generation of young Africans need to read.

Where the Bodies Are Buried

Sophie Gitonga

You've been watching him for two days now, waiting for the right time to grab him, but that time hasn't presented itself. Maybe it will today. He comes out of his house in a state of undress, shirt slung over his shoulder and trousers sagging dangerously. He looks the part of a thug. The driver waiting in a car outside his place revs the engine, drawing excitement from the children playing nearby. When your target gets in, the driver speeds off stirring up dust as dogs scamper for safety. You follow.

A call comes through: it's your boss.

"Falcon, what's the hold up?" he asks before you can get the phone to your ear.

"Nothing boss, I'm picking him up today."

"You've already been on this case for two days. I thought you were the best."

You hate it when people who sit behind a desk all day pretend they know how to do your job.

"Get it done!" he barks then hangs up. There's an unspoken ultimatum in there, but you don't care. Your boss is a vast and haughty man who thinks he's important because he has a direct line to the President. Well, he doesn't scare you.

The driver stops at a petrol station, one of those with the ubiquitous pizza and fried chicken outlets. You think they are here to get some food, but they don't get out of the car. You park right behind them and watch. Your target bobs his head to the blaring music as he chews miraa. That reminds you: you have some of your own. You retrieve it from under your seat. On nights like this, when you're not sure how long you'll be working, it's important to have something that will keep you alert. You watch as two other fellows get into the car. Their arrival causes the music in the car to turn way up. They drive off.

You hope this will not be another night of aimless driving and that at some point he will be alone long enough for you to get close to him. You follow them for ten kilometres as they weave in and out of traffic, sometimes driving right in the middle of a two-way street and forcing oncoming traffic to get off the road. Eventually, they come to a nondescript shopping centre, the kind with shops that have funny names: Morning Glory Milk Point, Wa Bens Cereals, Pewa Baby Pub. They park in front of the pub. When they open the doors of the car, smoke pours at their feet like fog. They are laughing and tripping over their own feet as they walk into the pub. You park in the shadows where your car is concealed, open the glove compartment and take out your pistol and its magazine.

The carousing is in full swing when you walk into the bar. The target is sitting at one end of the bar shouting orders to the waiter. You pick a table by the exit and sit in a way that ensures your eyes are always on him. You reach for some miraa stems in your jacket pocket, signalling to the waiter with your raised hand. He doesn't see you.

He whizzes by like a wound-up toy, balancing glasses, bottles of vodka and ginger ale on a tray. He wipes their table hurriedly and sets down the drinks. The target pulls a cigarette out of his pocket, lights it up and takes a long, satisfying drag.

"I'm sorry you can't smoke in here," the waiter says as he opens the soda bottle with a quick flick of the hand.

"Is this your mother's bar?" the target asks

"No."

"Then shut up!"

The waiter looks at him, then quickly turns on his heel. You raise your hand to get his attention, but his eyes are fixed on the floor. He's humiliated.

He returns with four glasses which he wipes with a tea towel that looks like it's also used to wipe the floor. He doesn't do a very good job of drying the glasses. As he leaves, he knocks the table with his hip tipping one of the open bottles and it spills onto the target's lap.

"Pole boss," he says as he dabs the target's lap with the tea towel.

"Are you stupid?" The target grabs his shirt collar and without warning, punches the waiter across the mouth. The commotion brings the place to silence. The waiter is holding his mouth which is now bleeding. The blood oozes past his fingers and onto the floor. The owner comes out from behind the counter, looks the waiter over and confronts the target.

"I'm going to have to ask you to leave," he says as he looks back at the waiter who is now holding a bloody incisor in his hand.

"Either sit the fuck down or I'll blow you the fuck away." The target is now pointing a gun at the owner. Things have escalated rather quickly. You feel your coat pocket for your gun. You are ready for anything.

"Okay let's all remain calm," the owner says. "Why don't I get you another round of drinks."

"On the house?"

"That's exactly what I meant."

The target looks at his friends, asking them if he should accept the offer or just shoot the guy and take over the bar. They laugh hysterically like he has said the funniest thing ever said by anyone past or present.

"How about you buy all the drinks we are going to have tonight and I won't have to kill you?"

The owner, defeated, acquiesces. He takes his wounded waiter with him, telling him to get cleaned up. He still has to work.

When he comes back out, you signal him. You still want a drink. His eyes are red. He's been crying. His upper lip is the size of a well-fed caterpillar.

After he brings your drink, he takes a seat by the TV and stares into the grainy screen. Is he really watching it or is he so traumatized that he's not really there? Every so often the target and his goons burst into raucous laughter; the waiter turns to look at them then returns to the TV. He's irritated and knows there's not a damn thing he can do about it.

The crowd ebbs and flows as the night wears on; you are only on your second drink and your eyes haven't left him. One of his friends appears to be asleep, his head hanging low like a banana plant heavy with fruit. The target pushes him, and he slides to the ground where he stays as the others look on, their own eyes at half-mast. The target steps over the sleeping one and announces that he's going to take a leak and they should be ready to go when he returns. They don't move or say anything. This could be your only chance, so you place a note under your beer bottle and follow him. You don't see him at first, but you hear the unmistakable sound of urine hitting the hard ground and you follow it. And behold, there he is, urinating right next to your car because of the privacy the darkness offers. You walk up next to him and say something about the beautiful cloudless night and the twinkling stars. He turns to look upward, exposing his neck. You strike with a swift chop, and he falls with a thud. You reach for the gun tucked in his waistband.

✝

The kill site is tucked deep in the woods; it would take anyone looking for him a month of Sundays to find him. You found it a few years ago when you were scouting for a place to dispose of the bodies without having to worry about a herds boy stumbling on them. Karura forest is too busy with joggers and dogs these days, and Nairobi river was recently cordoned off after a dredging exercise led to the discovery of the bodies of fourteen young men who had disappeared, over the years, under mysterious circumstances. The human rights people shouted themselves hoarse after the discovery, calling for 'swift investigations' and all that nonsense. Funny how they are concerned about human rights until some thug is pointing a gun at their faces. Then they start talking about the soaring crime rates and police laxity.

✝

He's coming to now, hacking like a dog with a bone lodged in its throat.

"Who are you?" he asks as he snatches breathes of air. He kicks the back doors of your car with all the effort he can muster, but they don't budge. He tries his feet at the partition between you until he tires. You watch him in the rear-view mirror as he tries, with handcuffs, to feel his pocket for his phone and wallet. You turned off his phone and put it and his wallet in the glove compartment.

"There's no way out so you might as well relax," you say.

The car's back seats were removed so it has a long trunk space and the back doors have no handles. And all the windows are tinted black. Simply put, your car is a hearse.

"Did Mwamba send you? Look, I already told him, he'll have to wait until next week to get his money. The police are on my case so I can't move the ...."

"Where did you go to school?"

"The fuck?"

"Your file doesn't include much about your early life so I'm curious."

"My file? Look man, I don't know who the hell you are or what you think you are doing. I suggest you let me out here before I make trouble for you. I know some cops who will fuck you up."

You stop the car, put the gear in park, but keep the engine still running. You step out and walk towards the back and open the boot door. He's smiling and saying something about how it's a good thing you have come to your senses. You whip him across the face with your pistol, cutting his lower lip. He's stunned.

"Guess what you little shit, I'm going to fuck you up."

You push him back in and slam the door shut. He is quiet for a long time after that, but not indefinitely, of course.

"You're a cop? Take me to the station then; I know my rights."

"Your rights huh?" You laugh. "You're not under arrest. We are just going on a little ride so I can get to know you."

"This is stupid. Who is your OCS? I want to talk to..."

"Tell me about your childhood, where did you grow up? I want to understand how you became a thug."

He's quiet, like he's plotting something, maybe looking for an escape route. You would do the same if you were him.

"Look, the sooner you tell me, the sooner we can be done with this night," you tell him reassuringly.

He begins talking. He tells you about growing up in Majengo, how he was born in a prison hospital because his mother had been jailed for soliciting and prostitution. He never knew his father, nor did he care to know him. He was probably a two-bit john who got his thrills from having condomless sex with prostitutes. His life wasn't great, growing up in the slum, but he was bright and got a pretty decent grade in his primary school national exams, which earned him a full scholarship to one of the national schools.

"My mother was so happy like it was her success too. That woman was out there busy selling her wares while I did the studying. I was happy to leave her."

As he talks about his mother, thoughts of your own mother emerge in the periphery of your mind. Growing up, you weren't exactly a good kid and you were far less intelligent than this guy. But for your mother, you would have ended up like this guy. She would rap your fingers with a ruler's edge when you stepped out of line and hug you so tightly immediately after, all the while whispering apologies in your ear. When she found out you were dyslexic, she insisted on hiring a teacher's aide to help you so you wouldn't fall behind. You wonder what she would think of you if she knew the tangent your career had taken.

"...anyway, I was caught with some sachets of vodka, one day. I told them they could keep their scholarship. They wanted me to slash grass in the school sports field for a week," he is saying.

"What happened after you dropped out?"

"I came back to the city to make some money. I was a street hawker for a little while, but the money was too kidogo and I had to find something more lucrative."

"Drugs you mean?"

"At first, yeah."

He was seventeen at the time and got into it first as a drug runner moving merchandise between towns. His school uniform served as a perfect disguise; no one would ever suspect a schoolboy of carrying kilos of drugs in his metal suitcase. After that, he moved to selling drugs on the street, but that was short-lived because he got involved in a turf war with another dealer.

"So I killed him," he says nonchalantly as if he were talking about killing an insect. "Wasn't it Darwin who said it's a jungle out here?" he asks.

"Perhaps you should have stayed in school a little longer," you say, truly sad for him

"Naah, wasn't for me?"

"And the rapes?'

He tells you he hasn't raped anyone; every encounter he's had was purely consensual. So you ask him about the fourteen-year-old, the one he beat to within an inch of her life.

"Oh is that what this is about? Her father sent you to avenge her? I'll tell you what I told that stupid mzee – his daughter came to me. She wanted it as much as I did."

"Why did you beat her?"

"Her father did that to her. Anyway, it's not important."

"So what is?"

"You tell me. You're the kidnapper," he scoffs.

"There was the guy you shot in his driveway."

"Which one, you'll have to remind me," he says offhandedly.

You tell him which one.

"Ah, that guy thought he was Rambo. I told him to just give me the keys. After all the car was insured, so he could get himself another one."

"You killed him and maimed his wife!" you say.

He denies any responsibility. He says the victim lunged at him and tried to wrestle the gun away from him, so he shot in defence.

He prattles on about his other killings, his excitement building with each retelling. You ask him if he feels remorse. He ponders your question only briefly before saying, "Everybody dies".

"So where are you taking me? You've been driving quite a while," he asks.

You tell him to relax that you are about to get there. He says he needs to relieve himself. You tell him he'll have to hold it in.

"Are you going to kill me?"

You don't answer immediately; you let the question hang out there like laundry still damp days after being washed.

"Do you think you deserve to die?"

"Stop toying with me, you bastard. If you are a man, then kill me here and now," he taunts.

He starts kicking the partition between you with one foot then brings in the other, slowly at first then increased his speed. You drive on, unperturbed. He starts cackling.

"Consider me a mirror," he says as he licks spittle at the corners of his mouth.

"What does that mean?"

"It means you and I are the same. Only difference is, you're a mercenary for the state."

He's not wrong, at least not on one count. Publicly, the government has condemned your activities going as far as promising to take action against officers "who take the law into their own hands". With mounting pressure from foreign envoys, the Minister of Internal Security even disbanded your squad a few months ago. But away from everyone's view, it's business as usual, with full government backing. Perhaps it helps that the boss has a direct line with the President. But your target is also wrong: the people you kill are not good people. They are ruthless rapists, drug dealers, and murderers who upend lives without batting an eye. They bribe their way out of accountability and strut around feeling untouchable. Even their mothers would agree that they are better off dead. You press a little harder on the accelerator.

"Did I touch a nerve?" he asks and laughs again. "I know what you are thinking. You are convincing yourself that what you do is about restoring law and order. I say that's bullshit."

He swallows, thirst now kicking in after all that alcohol.

"If you really cared about justice and all that, then you'd arrest me properly and take me to court."

"You are right. I don't care about justice. I care about getting a job done once and right."

You see his eyes widen in the rear-view mirror. What a kid!

"You'd just bribe your way out of there before the ink on the charge sheet even dried," you say. "And I don't have no time for arresting you shits over and over."

"Then why not arrest the judge as well? Better still; why not kill him too?"

He is burning with righteous anger at the injustice of it all.

"Thanks for the tip, I'll take that under advisement," you say and long for a cigarette although you stopped smoking ages ago.

Him being quiet after all that yammering makes you restless for some reason, but he is not one for long silences. He is used to being heard. "What was it like the first time you killed someone?"

They all ask this, and you've never understood why.

The details of your own first kill are committed to memory, down to what you were wearing. It took you about ten minutes to kill the guy. You had your hands around his throat with the express intent of strangling him to death. An amateur mistake. You should have just shot him. The guy put up a spirited fight, at one point biting you and then taking off despite his hands being handcuffed behind his back. When you finally caught up to him, you slammed him to the ground and used a rock to bash his face in. You don't remember how many blows you delivered. The end result was not pretty, and you became violently ill. It haunted you for a while after that, how angry you were when he tried to get away from you, how satisfied you felt when you smashed his face in. It awakened something both primal and unsavoury within you, something whose embers you've been trying to put out since that very first day.

"It was alright," is all you say to your target, and the conversation fades into an uncomfortable silence.

✝

You pull up to the kill site and you park so that the headlights point down the sloping path. You get out of the car, walk to the rear and open the boot door, lifting it up above your head. He doesn't move. You shine a torch at his face; his lower lip is swollen and jutting out like a pier into the ocean. You motion with the torch that he should disembark. He does so slowly.

"What happens now?" he asks, sounding like a child. You realize then that despite all his bravado, he really is just a boy. And standing next to you, he could be your boy. But you know better than to get sentimental. It's not about whose child he is; even the people he hurt were other people's children.

"Now we walk," you tell him and put your hand on his shoulder tightly as you light the path in front of him.

"Gently bana!" He shakes his shoulder to get free from your grip. You let him go.

"What is this place?" he asks, but you don't answer. He stumbles a couple of times. It's fine that he stumbles, you are not in a hurry.

"Is this where the bodies are buried?"

You offer nothing, and he looks back at you expectantly. Realizing that there's nothing more to be said, he sits on the ground abruptly like a mule burdened by a heavy load and that will go no further. You tell him to get up, but he doesn't. He makes you an offer: he'll double whatever they are paying you if you let him go. You tell him to get up. He'll triple it or make you a partner in his deals. You'd like that, wouldn't you? To be a shareholder in a very lucrative venture? You are unmoved. You lift him by his belt, and he starts to plead with you, his voice shaky with desperation. He makes a new offer. He will confess to all his crimes in exchange for a jail sentence and also tell you the names of all his associates, including the cops. Or he could just leave town, which would be just as good, right? No one would ever have to know; it would be just between you and him. He turns around forcefully, and you think he's going to pounce on you or try to make a run for it, but he kneels and lifts his head to look at you. He's crying now, and he lets his tears flow freely. What a change from the cocky bastard he was only a couple of hours ago. His eyes are searching your face for the slightest hint of mercy, but you give him nothing. You have a job to do and a boss to answer to.

"Let's go."

You help him up and lead him the rest of the way down the hill.

Sophie Gitonga has been writing on and off since she was a child but decided to become serious about it this past decade. Her writing projects cover diverse topics including current affairs, entrepreneurship, and travel, although her absolute favourites are food and unrequited love. Connect with her on twitter as @sophiehmk

Wife Material

Shiru Waweru

Maina had swiped right on almost every girl on the app. He'd been trying to find a date unsuccessfully for the past year and had joined Tinder as a last-ditch effort. His friends were all paired up, and he was often lonely, especially when they had group plans. He would never admit it to them, but he resented the fact that they no longer spent concentrated time with him. A girlfriend was always involved.

He didn't know why finding a girlfriend was proving so hard; he was smart, had a good job and was old enough to be considered serious about settling down. He was getting tired of coming home to an empty house and having his meals alone.

"Isn't that a hook up app?" he'd asked, when his friends had suggested Tinder.

"Yeah, and?"

"I'm looking for wife material."

"I still don't see the problem. Keep up with the times, man; people can meet anywhere these days."

Because they spoke highly of the app and because they were doing much better than him in the dating department, he signed up against his better judgement. He decided that he wouldn't mention it to them unless he successfully met someone suitable. Furthermore, if his idiotic friends could convince rational females to go out with them and keep going out with them, he at least stood a chance.

Maina put his phone down and went to make himself a drink at the mahogany bar he had recently set up in his living room, but before he had unscrewed the bottle of gin, his phone dinged, indicating that he had matched with someone on the app. He abandoned the drink and wiped his sweaty palms on his pants.

He'd matched with five girls.

He was ecstatic – the fact that he'd swiped on over fifty girls notwithstanding. He immediately began drafting a text to his matches, afraid if he didn't do something right away, they would disappear. He figured it would be harmless to send them all the same text. Not wanting to seem too eager when they did reply, he left his phone on the coffee table, went to his closet and took out five shirts in order of his most favourite to his least favourite. He saved his best shirt for the girl who would interest him the most. He then took out five pairs of slacks and paired them with the shirts. He took off his clothes and stood in front of his full-length mirror trying to figure out what had appealed to his matches. He flexed his biceps and turned from side to side. Or maybe it was his burgeoning beard that had attracted the five ladies. He tried a couple of 'sexy' looks and smirks in the mirror and then dropped onto the bed, already seeing his dates play out on the ceiling above him. This was going to be fun.

The next day, Maina met one of his five matches after work at a local cafe. He ordered a glass of water, drank it down and ordered another. When she arrived, she sat down with her phone in hand, constantly texting as she peppered him with questions. The date was awkward, and Maina was a little irritated by the end. He felt he should have taken charge of the date and led the conversation. Instead, he'd let her ask him questions as if he were the one who needed to prove himself.

Bitch.

He went on his second date the next day at the same cafe. He didn't like to spend too much on first dates because they didn't always guarantee results. He vowed to be more forward; girls liked that. He needed to be an alpha and make her want to submit to him. He took a whiskey shot to calm his nerves and waited… and waited. He took another shot. Half an hour later, he texted her and got no reply. He had been stood up. So far Tinder was proving to be full of the exact kind of woman he didn't want.

The waitress brought him his bill and smiled at him sweetly. She seemed nice, but he reminded himself that waitresses were not wife material. Not with their infamous reputation.

✝

Maina didn't get back on Tinder for a week and when he did, he scrutinized his third match's profile more carefully. Her body looked good, but her top was too tight, her skirt too short and her makeup too much. She looked like the kind of girl who liked to trap men with her looks. He preferred a girl with a more natural look; this one seemed too worldly. He decided that he would wait and see how the other dates played out before asking number three out.

The pressure to settle down was getting out of hand. His mother had called him again that afternoon asking him to bring his girlfriend home for the holidays. The problem was that he hadn't told her that he'd broken up with Mingina six months before. She had left him for a taller, richer, buffer version of himself, exactly what Nairobi women wanted these days. There was no hope for guys like him who were nice but didn't fit the physical requirements. Mingina had taught him that lesson in the harshest way possible. That new guy was probably going to cheat on her and beat her up, but she thought she'd upgraded.

Whore.

The next time he went to the cafe, to wait out Nairobi traffic, he found himself on the lookout for the waitress who had served him the last time, despite his reservations. She recognized him from across the room and smiled that gorgeous smile, walking up to his table.

They should hire more girls like her.

"No one to stand you up this time?" she asked as she took his order.

He tensed before he realized she was teasing and let out a laugh. "I learnt my lesson."

"Dating in this Nairobi seems like hell."

Maina's stomach went cold. Was she married? "So you're not dating?"

"I don't have much time. I've had to work since I finished primary school."

He noticed that she was lingering, pretending to be arranging the condiments on the table. She was interested.

"Me too," he said. "I have to take care of my younger siblings."

She gave him her full attention now, clearly full of admiration. "Wow. That must have been hard."

Maina felt understood and seen for who he really was, a nice, decent person. When she went off to get his coffee, she left him beaming.

Now there was a woman who knew all about hard work and had not gotten her head full of crazy Nairobi ideas. He wanted to wait until her shift ended and talk to her some more, but he thought this would make her think he had nothing to do and was a pushover. When she brought the bill, he asked her for her number and left her a large tip. He hoped that would indicate his interest and his financial stability.

He kept staring at her number on his phone the next three days but did not call her until the fourth day, not wanting to give her the idea that he was desperate. He thought of taking her somewhere nice but settled on a café on the other side of town from her workplace – best to keep her expectations low for now.

At the café, he took charge, signalled the waiter and placed their orders, assuring her she would like the food he was ordering. He was paying, after all, and she seemed amenable to letting him decide. He was glad that she had agreed to the date immediately, proving that she was not one to play silly games.

As they chatted, he noticed that she kept pulling on the ends of her shirt, which in turn emboldened him, and he tried to joke around a bit to make her feel more at ease. He was finally in his element; she was simple, humble and didn't talk too much.

He felt more relaxed than he had with any of his other dates. Moraa was sweet and attentive and listened to him intently, making him feel as though he was the only person in her world right then. She was eager to learn from him. He was so relieved, and he found himself leaning forward to get to know her more. But at the back of his mind, he was worried that she would be just like his ex and decide that she could do better than him.

Relax. You're getting ahead of yourself.

He couldn't afford to lose this one before he even got into the game.

"So what else do you do?" he finally asked, realizing he was talking too much about himself.

She fidgeted with a napkin on the table. "I work in theatre in my free time. I make props."

Maina smiled. "That's so cool! What's the last thing you made?"

She hesitated. "A prop knife. I make them so that the blade retracts into the hilt."

"Fascinating. I'd love to see one."

She gave him an eager smile and looked like a happy puppy, then removed a knife from her bag. She went into detail about how she sourced her material and how she made them look so real. It was clear prop-making was something she liked doing. And that endeared her to him even more.

"You just carry this with you?"

"It's just a habit I've formed over the years. I get really into whatever I'm making at the moment, so I usually have a sample with me at all times."

He took the knife from her and tested the blade. "You're good. This looks like the real deal." He played with it again before handing it back to her.

"I carry a switchblade with me," he said, removing the blade from his pocket. "Habit."

She studied the blade intently before giving it back to him. All her movements were delicate and cute. He was glad that they had knives in common. It would make things so much easier.

"I had a really nice time, Maina," she said outside the café. "It's been a while since I met anyone serious." She paused. "So where to from here?"

Maina was a bit taken aback because he hadn't planned that far ahead, but he recovered quickly and invited her over to his place, some few kilometres away and ten minutes via Uber. As soon as they were inside and he locked the door, she pounced on him, kissing him and simultaneously undoing the buttons on his shirt. Maina was surprised for the second time that day but not enough to want to stop, even though he wondered about her giving it up on the first date.

The sex was satisfactory, however. Maina felt he had outdone himself.

"Woah. What's that?" said Moraa, wrapping a sheet around her body. She slipped out of bed and walked over to the display case at the opposite end of the bedroom.

"A hobby of mine," Maina preened.

Moraa reached into the display case and pulled out a delicate stiletto knife with a wooden handle. She turned it over in her hands, examining the craftsmanship. "It's beautiful."

"That was a groomsman gift during a friend's wedding."

"That's a thing?" she asked, replacing the stiletto and picking up a bench made Casbah blade. "Oh wow, they even personalized them. That's my kind of gift."

Maina could barely contain himself. She was the one. He could already hear wedding bells. He walked over and picked up an exquisite, rainbow Flomascus folding knife.

"Here." He handed it to her.

"It's gorgeous." She flipped it open and ran the blade over her wrist.

"You can have it."

"There's no way I'm taking this."

"Take it. It's too girly for me." He corrected the placement of the stiletto in the case.

When he turned back to her, she kissed him, and they ended up in bed once more.

"I want to try something."

"What?" Moraa sat up.

"Knife-play, have you tried it before?"

"No … I mean yes, but it didn't end well."

Maina smiled. "I promise you'll like it."

She bit her lip in that innocent way of hers. "I'll try it if you show me how you like it."

He felt ten feet tall and looked deep into her trusting eyes as he demonstrated by gently running the Flomascus across her collarbone without once drawing blood.

She took the blade from him and tried to run it down his chest, but he held her by the wrist. "I do the playing."

She straddled him and handed him the knife. And Maina, not one to be accused of being a killjoy, took the knife from her hand and gently ran the blade down her chest, between her breasts. He studied the knife as though he'd never seen it before, and then he repeated the motion on his own chest. Pleasure ripped through him.

Certain that he wouldn't cause her any harm, he drew her down and kissed her. And when he eventually thrust himself inside her, he ran the blade all over her chest and abdomen, sometimes drawing blood. She didn't seem to notice. He licked the blood off her and continued thrusting. When she finally peaked, he couldn't have been prouder.

✝

A month later, Maina met up with his boys. He was eager to tell them about Moraa, but he knew they would make fun of him for being so enamoured with a girl he had just met, especially one

172

who had given it up so quickly. He would have to leave that part out.

"The wife has been bugging me lately. Ati she wants me to spend more time with the kids," Joseh said.

"Mine wants me to let her go on one of those girls' nights out. We all know what happens there," Kim piped up.

These were common complaints his friends often brought up. It seemed their wives were nagging and didn't know how to let them lead. They kept telling Maina to make sure he picked a nice quiet girl, preferably one who would defer to him on big decisions and understood that he was the head of the house. That was the only way to make a marriage work. Kim felt that his wife had stopped respecting him as soon as she had received a promotion; she was now earning more than him and that was making her big-headed. Joseh felt that his was getting lazy and was making demands on him to get involved in jobs that were very clearly hers, like child-rearing.

Maina had heard all of this before, but he couldn't see Moraa being the type of girl to be disrespectful. From what he'd learnt about her, she'd been raised right and was disciplined. She was definitely wife material.

†

The play was rather boring, and yet this was the most animated he had seen Moraa. She talked about the gruelling weeks leading up to opening night, letting him know that she had played a huge role in the play coming together the way it had.

"What do you think?" she whispered expectantly.

"It's good."

After the curtain closed, she insisted on taking Maina backstage for a tour and to meet some of the cast.

"Moraa! Oh my God, the set looks amazing!" said one of them.
She grinned stupidly. "Doesn't it? I'm so proud."
"Who was that?" Maina asked.
"You don't recognize him? He was the main actor."
"I'm a man. I'm inclined to pay more attention to women."
She gave him a strange look but wisely didn't make the comment he could see on her lips.

All the cast members she introduced him to gushed over her work, and Maina felt as though she had orchestrated this whole tour as an excuse just to brag. It was unattractive. She wasn't even paying him any mind and forgot to introduce him five different times. How hard could it possibly be to make a fake knife? Surely some of these people were overdoing it. Like the guy who stood a little too close to her. He gave her a peck on the cheek.

"You've outdone yourself. What would we be without you?"

Simp.

Maina stood with his hand on the nape of her neck, grinning and feeling lost as they discussed more fake items.

"And who was that?" he asked when the creep finally went away.
"My friend, the play director."
"He couldn't have dressed properly for his own play?"
"Babe, he's an artist."

She was acting strange and defensive. This side of her he did not like very much. She wouldn't be continuing with the prop-making if they got married. "Are you done?" he asked.

"No. I'm going out to celebrate with the cast."
"And him?"
"Well, he is part of the cast, so yes."
"Where?"
"I don't know yet."
"You guys hadn't planned?"

"God, Maina. You're always so suspicious. Come with us. They are fun people."

"No thanks."

An ugly crease appeared between her eyebrows. "I think you should trust me."

"And I think this is the kind of thing we should talk about beforehand."

"Okay then, let's talk when I get back. I'll come to your place."

There was more to say, but she was smiling beautifully at him. She really was his weakness. He gave in. "Okay, but don't keep me waiting for too long."

His night went downhill from there. Moraa texted a couple of hours later letting him know that she would, in fact, be staying out later than agreed and that she would see him another day. He didn't appreciate these so-called friends of hers, and he certainly wouldn't condone being disrespected like that.

Maina deliberately avoided contacting her, hoping that she would see she was on the wrong, but three days went by, and Moraa didn't call to apologize. Finally, on the fourth day, he was so pissed off, he called her. She didn't pick up.

I knew it.

He refused to be made a fool of a second time, so the next day he went to Moraa's place, planning to get the truth out of her. As soon as she opened the door, she threw her arms around his neck and apologized over and over. He was taken aback.

"You just made me so angry, talking to me like that," she said.

He didn't want to fight. Not with her body pressed up on his. He kissed her and she led him straight to her bedroom. But he didn't let her make him forget.

Afterwards, he walked around her house, looking at everything carefully, searching for evidence. She must have thought he was admiring her mismatched collection of furniture because she said, "Most of these are hand-me-downs from my aunt."

He turned to her sharply. "Where did you sleep that night?"

"Gosh. Here. I took a cab." That crease on her brow again. "How can we make a relationship work if you can't even trust me?" She sat down not looking at him. "I've done nothing wrong and I'm being punished."

"I told you not to be late and you decided not to come over at all, and yes, you're being punished."

"I'm not a child, Maina."

"Then don't act like one."

So dramatic this one.

She suddenly went to the kitchen and brought him a plate of food, and he accepted it for the apology it was, although part of him wondered at her abrupt change of mind.

Then he realized he was succeeding. He was slowly moulding her into a proper wife.

✝

But several weeks later, Moraa told him that she couldn't sleep over because she needed to get back to work. Her mother was sick, and she had to find a way to get her father the money for the hospital bills. Maina tried to convince her to stay over on the promise that he would help her family out, but she wouldn't budge.

"I just can't live off of you. You know I'm not like that," she said, a tad too angrily.

He took a deep breath to control himself. "Let me drive you at least."

"No, it's late." she said. "You've had a long day. I'll fix you something when I get back." She smiled like a wonderful thing opening up.

He called her a cab, instead, but wasn't happy. He walked back up to his apartment, nursing disappointment and some anger. If he and Moraa were going to start a life together, it was important that she understood he would take care of her and her family. It was his duty as her man. She probably felt the need to act independent so he wouldn't think she was after his money, which he liked about her, but he needed to clarify his role in their lives. That was a conversation they would have soon and which he intended to win.

Not long after Moraa had left, one of Maina's friends, Joseh, called to invite him out for a drink. Maina wasn't in the mood for more of Joseh's complaining about the wife, but he had nothing else to do. They met up outside the Joseh's local pub. And as soon as they walked in, Maina's heart turned to stone. He recognized the sway of the hips of one of the waitresses.

"Moraa?" He looked down at the short skirt the servers were required to wear and her tight shirt and felt rage swell within him.

Liars, all of them.

She had the good sense to look guilty but was hardly apologetic. She tried to dodge: "Babe, I'll come over and serve you just now."

Maina left her without a word and went to join Joseh, seething as he waited for her to serve them. If Joseh had noticed the altercation, he did not seem to have understood.

"Now that's a body. Taking her home?" he asked, visibly salivating over Moraa.

Maina was rethinking everything and was glad that he hadn't talked to his friends about her, because he would be looking like a big fool now. He watched her all night as she flirted with patrons and laughed with them.

Slut.

"Look at her," Joseh sneered sometime later, gesturing to where Moraa was disengaging herself from a patron's drunken embrace. The man put a bill in her front pocket and quickly grazed her boob before sending her off to the bar with another order. "They are all bitches. The ones you marry and the ones you don't."

Maina couldn't disagree, the evidence was damning. It would seem he had not made himself to clear to Moraa, a mistake he couldn't wait to correct.

He timed his exit with the end of Moraa's shift. He waved Joseh off, promising to call him later in the week and waited for her in the parking lot. They drove back to his house in silence. He watched her through the corner of his eye, thinking terrible things, especially because she did not look at all remorseful; quiet, innocent, yes, but not sorry for embarrassing him that way. Well, he was not an idiot, and he would make sure she understood it. He banged the door of his apartment shut when she was inside.

"You lied to me?" he said, trying to control his anger.

"What do you want to hear, Maina? I really need this money," she said, settling on the couch with nonchalance and taking up the T.V.'s remote controller.

He stood between her and the T.V. "And did you also need to let all those men touch you?"

"It's not like I enjoy it. That's how men treat waitresses. Why are you being like this?"

He took a step forward, and she leaned back into the couch, wide-eyed, apparently finally understanding that he was very pissed. But then she stood up and headed for the kitchen, throwing the human hair weave he had bought for her birthday present, over her shoulder, at him. Him!

"So you just let other men touch what's mine?" Something akin to scorn flashed in her eyes, but it was gone so fast he thought he had imagined it. "Answer me!"

She didn't, her arms now folded over her chest, with arrogance.

Maina's voice rose. "You'd rather whore yourself out even when I have so graciously offered to help."

"I'm not a whore!" Her mouth contorted as if she was speaking to a dirty and persistent beggar.

Maina couldn't take it anymore and before the action even registered, he had slapped her hard across the face. She stumbled against the kitchen counter. He made her look at him, pulling her head by the hair. "I am not your toy."

Still, he saw defiance in her eyes and punched it away with a blow from his fist. Her head hit the cabinet above the marble counter, and she slipped to the floor and held herself tightly, defensively.

"Look what you made me do!" he yelled.

He paced the kitchen as she cried softly in the corner.

"Oh God," he said, adrenaline coursing through his body. "If you had just talked to me, if you had just listened, none of this would have happened." He wanted to shake her, to make her see her ungratefulness. He kicked a stool she'd insisted he buy for his kitchen. He knew he needed to calm down, but he was a tornado well on its course. He wanted to tear down everything. She would be the ruin of him. He had known it all along, but stupidly thought...

"I'm... I'm sorry, Maina," she said, suddenly hugging his legs.

His anger broke, and he saw what he had done. Oh God, her face was swollen, and she was bleeding on one cheek. He immediately took her in his arms and hugged her. "I'm sorry, baby. I would never hurt you on purpose, you know that, right?" He didn't wait for her response. "I'm only this way because of how strong my feelings for you are. It drives me crazy. I've never felt like this for anyone. Don't you understand?" He kept rubbing circles around her back to soothe her.

She leaned into him for a long time, crying and shaking a little, vulnerable. He so wanted to protect her, especially from herself. Didn't she see how good they were together? When she left his warm embrace, she gave him a small reconciliatory smile. "I'll go make you a drink," she said.

And Maina let out a breath he hadn't even known he was holding. He'd almost messed up. Oh God! He was not a woman-beater. She wasn't good for him, no, she wasn't.

She fixed him a gin and tonic and took it to him where he sat at the edge of the couch, unable to relax.

"I'm sorry, Maina." She knelt humbly by his feet.

They sat silent for a while. He stared at the black T.V. screen, at the man she had made him. He was keenly aware of her hand caressing his, like the licks of a cat's tongue.

"What can I do, babe?" she asked.

He could not speak.

"Let me make it up to you, Maina." She grabbed her purse and retrieved the Flomascus blade that he'd given her. "Let me make you feel good." She took her clothes off and stroked herself with the knife right there in the sitting room. "Let me use my present on you."

No, she is just perfect for me.

He took a swig of his drink and placed the glass on a side table, indicating his acquiescence. He wanted to forget the whole episode. She took his clothes off expertly and laid him on the couch. She straddled him and began gyrating her hips against his crotch while simultaneously stroking him with the knife. It was strange for him to have her in charge, but it was also powerfully arousing. He was glad they were trying it this way. Maybe this was what she needed in order for her to let him lead in other important things. He now thought that maybe he'd judged her too harshly. His friends had often accused him of being so rigid, but if they could see him now, they would know he was the most open-minded one of them all.

As she stroked away, he realized he was feeling drowsy, and the blade was biting into his skin harder than before, sharp and bruising.

"Wait," he attempted to say, but his tongue was heavy and slow, and he was choking on it. He coughed, and liquid slid down his cheek. He looked up at her through a fog. Her eyes were maniacal. And suddenly, his chest was wet, but he never sweated this much, not even when the elevator was down, and he had to take all ten flights of stairs to his apartment.

She lifted the knife, and he finally noticed the red film clinging to the blade. Then she buried the Flomascus into his chest one last time

Shiru Waweru studied Business and I.T. but is now a transcriber and a freelance writer. When she's not writing, she's singing, swimming or trying something new. This is her first published work. You can find more of her work on her blog simplywesh.wordpress.com. Connect with her on Twitter as @simply_wesh.

About the Nairobi Fiction Writing Workshop

NF2W is the only long-length, graduate-level fiction writing program in Kenya. It offers new and emerging writers an opportunity to intensely and extensively study the craft of fiction writing over a period of 16 to 18 weeks. For many of these writers, NF2W is the first and only engagement with formal fiction writing training. Therefore, to allow access to writers of all income levels, at least two to three writers in each NF2W session undertake the program on full need- and merit-based scholarships.

As of this publication, the NF2W writing community consists of forty budding writers – past and present participants of the workshop, as well as more experienced writers who have graciously agreed to join the community and share their knowledge.

Upon graduation, all participants are invited to submit a short story for publication in the NF2W annual digital anthology. Those who choose to do so, undertake several months of rewriting and editing, extending their in-class training through one-on-one sessions with the anthology editor. For many participants, stories appearing in the NF2W anthology are the first to ever be published.

Beyond disseminating formal fiction writing training to Kenya-based writers of all nationalities, genders, creeds, orientations, races, ideologies and other important identifiers, NF2W aims to provide Kenyan secondary and tertiary institutions with an example of how to incorporate the teaching of creative writing into their curriculums. Also, in the near future, NF2W hopes to launch a mentoring program, connecting its graduates with experienced writers anywhere in the world who are willing to act as mentors on writing and publishing. Furthermore, part of the proceeds of this anthology will be used as prize money in an annual short story contest to launch in 2020 with the aim of giving talented Kenya, and later African, writers the resources they need to seriously pursue writing.

If interested in participating in, partnering with or donating any resources to the Nairobi Fiction Writing Workshop, please contact Makena Onjerika at makenaonjerika@gmail.com.